The Musician

Cover by
Brina Williamson

Disclaimer:

All characters and situations portrayed in this work are purely fictional
and any resemblance to persons or events either living or dead
is entirely coincidental.

To order additional copies, please see our estore at:
www.createspace.com/3577000

The Musician

2011

KERRI BENNETT WILLIAMSON

The Musician

TABLE OF CONTENTS

ACKNOWLEDGEMENTS:

Special appreciation is due to my darling husband (the wondrous genius of a man who keeps my computer in line and online), my beloved sons and daughters (who are each blessed with far greater writing talent and skill than I could ever hope to possess), and my closest family and friends for their generous encouragement and support.

Particular gratitude belongs with my daughter Brina for her magnificent cover art: this book could never shine from a shelf without her artistic brilliance. Many thanks also go out to my readers around the world for all their complimentary and supportive emails through www.bonnetsandaprons.com and www.wizarts.biz (as well as the recently new www.kerribennettwilliamson.com and now www.austenbronte.com).

DEDICATION:

To all musicians who compose or play music that blesses any audience the world over: whether to comfort sorrows or to lift spiritually.

1
Music

Walking along, on my way through that part of town to pick up some work, was when I first heard it. There was music in the air. That hauntingly beautiful song would become as if my very own from the first. Once I heard the piece enough times to know it well, the almost melancholy loveliness was very oftentimes playing in my head, or in my mind's ear, over and over again.

Seemingly lilting from beyond this mortal sphere, the notes called to me as if on a higher plane. The flowing tune wafted down from an upper window. I was transfixed to the melody, as well as to other melodious companion notes in attendance to the main theme. I found it difficult to continue walking. I did not wish to quickly pass by. Indeed, I stopped. I listened, completely.

That first composition sent down from an upper window of that house to my ears was as if a symphony, not that I had ever heard such an assemblage myself, but I knew enough about music to imagine symphonic harmony. I had heard many different musical instruments. I had heard some together at once. I had played at a few of them in my relatively distant past. I could picture the synchronization of a multiplicity of instruments playing as one.

There were at least two sets of melodies in that work of musical art, I came to find. The first time I heard the song playing, I only noticed the main theme or key melody, but it was that principle portion to the piece that spoke to and stirred my soul so fully from my first listen to it. The second time I walked past, and the musician was once more playing what I soon called my song, I more fully detected another melody: a secondary part to that musical piece. Both sides to that musical story spoke to me in an intensely deep way, though it was the predominant portion that seemed to be trancelike to my mind and spirit.

That particular song which I speak of was played with an intensity of feeling that moved me beyond my words to describe it. In that moment, I felt spiritually connected to the player somehow, as if he or she was my beloved brother or sister from a long ago and faraway place in heavenly days gone by: somebody from happy times in childhood perhaps, or somebody from my former blissful life before birth.

It was a piano. The musician was playing that exultant melody of mine on a piano. I had grown up playing a piano, though I did not actually have access to one now. I hadn't thought of piano-playing in what seemed years. At least the time since I yearned to play the piano again, seemed so very long ago. I hadn't even sung, save hymns at church, and I didn't tend to do much of that these days. I had lost the desire to go to church, let alone sing there or anywhere, for that matter.

Once the eloquent song had done its initial mystery upon me, I generally continued on my way. I tried to recall the tune in my mind. I ached to remember it. I wanted to hum it, but how can one hum a song aloud that tends to escape the musical avenues of the mind? I could not walk past that house again soon enough. I hoped for that song to play again. In point of fact, I even prayed for the musician to sit at that piano and play the melody once more, for me. I needed to hear it again; and again. I needed to know it. I could not know it well enough for my liking and remembering without hearing it many times. I was no musical genius.

Each time I ambled past that place, I could not leave the realm of that house and its music playing until I felt assured within myself that *my* beloved singular musical number had played, was completely finished, and when another, a different song, had begun. Whether I heard my own preferred piece firstly or what seemed finally, after numerous other songs, I did not desire leaving the close territory of that home until my song had played, and played itself out complete.

I begged the heavens for that musical wonder to be written upon my mind enough to be retrieved at any time that I might need it, to hold onto. Of course, as I have alluded to from the beginning, my prayers were answered: many times. I heard the song once more; and then many more times. It was not very long before I knew it. I could play at least the key part of the melody in my mind most any time. That song became my own lullaby at night, to rock myself to sleep to. I clung to it. It comforted me. It shared my burdens, or so it seemed to me that it did.

I could never play like that. Not on a piano, or any other instrument for that matter. I did not have the talent nor skill to ever play that well. Even with years of practice, I could not imagine ever playing any song so very well. I would have liked to try. If I had had a piano at my disposal, I would have tried. I wanted to try playing that song. I wanted to practice it with my hands until my fingers knew it far better than my waking mind.

As you might guess, I would find my way to walking past that house as many times as I could reasonably muster, day after day, and I would hope that the musician would grant me my wish each time. Many times I would be blessed to hear it again. That piece was touched on at least once daily, to be sure. I supposed that the musical composition that had so quickly come to mean so very much to me, must have meant a good deal to its player as well. Else why would the musician play that song so very often? Unless compelled by my prayers to do so? I could not discount anything.

But what was that captivating song? Did it have a known name? Who composed it? Who played it? Was the musician a man or a woman? Was the player the composer? Was there any story behind that melody? There seemed a good deal of sweetness and yet perhaps a little of some pain slightly hidden in the notes. It reminded me of how I felt about my own life: my pains, my regrets, my sorrows, and the richly deep joys that I did surely know throughout it all, and in spite of all that was not right with my life, at least for now.

Walking past that house, getting lost in the beautiful music that fell like an edifying waterfall from that upper window, particularly that one song; I seemed more able to cling to the joys that I was lucky enough to possess in this life. Yes, the song reminded me of my sorrows too, but I was somehow more able to forget the pain and sadness that I had known for too long, and far too oftentimes. The musician helped me to count my blessings instead of my woes, through that song.

There was more musically to love in the air near that house than that one favored melody of mine. There were other songs that drew me into that upper window. There were also other instruments. Over time, I heard more than a piano playing. I especially heard a violin as well. When the violin played, there seemed so much sadness and even agony attached to it. The violin cried out in a way, all the more so than the piano did.

It seemed to me that the musician turned to the violin when depression loomed. My heart ached with the player of those wavering strings during those times. I walked slower. I sank in spirit. I wondered what tragic history attended the bow over those strings. What could make a musician play with such great pain? I seldom could stop my own tears from flowing wildly when that violin played.

But my song, the piano song I shared with its player, still filled my heart and made my spirit soar, and ache, simultaneously every time I heard it. My tears would be pulled forth, my soul would feel sweetness: I seemed sad and happy all at once. When the fingers of that musician ran over the piano keys to play that composition, I could not help but wonder what that little and large musical miracle evoked in he or she who played it.

And so, day upon day, my life was nourished by that musician. I was lifted. I was filled with hope. I was fed. I was no longer as hungry as before. Yes, I felt my sorrows too, but I felt alive such as I had not done in so very long. I was no longer the walking dead that I had heretofore been in a way. I did not feel so terribly alone as I had been inclined to. I felt befriended in a way. Little did that pianist know all that was given to me through that music: whether piano, violin or another instrument. I wanted to thank that musician for enriching my own life. I wanted to meet that person, whoever they may be. I wished I could give back something in return for that valuable gift that I had received. The music had awakened me, from darkest night into daylight.

2
The House

Being a black and white Tudor style, the house reminded me of a piano with its black keys on white. It seemed an obvious thing to me. In fact, it was as much as almost striped in that recognizable way. The structure would have begged for a piano being played somewhere in it, if not for the musician being there to accommodate that obvious need.

I imagined that the house must have been chosen precisely for or by the musician. It seemed built for such a one. I quickly called it the piano house to myself once I'd heard the pianist's music flowing out if it, though I had never seen it as such prior. When the house had sat there quietly, all those times before the musician came to live and play there in it, it seemed simply another house that I walked past. I had barely noticed it.

It was definitely grander than the house I currently lived in, I should say, though I certainly lived in no hovel myself. However, the piano house was much larger than the one I had grown up in. I would not necessarily guess that those folk who now owned the house were excessively wealthy, but they could not possibly be poor to reside in such a place. They surely must have some ready money to afford it.

The piano house was not the grandest private residence in town, to be sure, nor was it set in the richest of neighborhoods. Now, I do not claim that there were true neighborhoods in town, but there were deviations of grandeur when it came to clusters of homes. The most impressive houses tended to reside in their own particular parts of town, with the poorest cabins outlying here and there in their little humble groups together, and then there were the little in-between varying sets of cottages and houses throughout the town and about. The sizes of the houses differed as did their little or larger plots of land.

The area of town where I lived was not so very different than where the musician lived. The house I called my current home was situated in a slightly more humble set of houses and in another part of town. I should not say humble, for I did not live in a humble house by any means, but the house where the piano played so gloriously was, I thought, a larger and more impressive house than the one that I resided in. I did not live afar off from the piano house. Of course, where I lived was certainly far enough distant that I could never hear the piano playing from the musician's window to my own. Thus, I found myself taking all my walks nearer to that house than I ever had done before that piano began playing. I rerouted my walks to include passing by the piano house.

This house that the musician resided in was somewhere on the way to stateliness, I should say, at least by my own estimation. I suppose that judgment would depend on the beholder. I considered it quite a nice and large home, but, as I have suggested already, I lived in a spaciously comfortable place myself. Others, those people who might call something more of a humble cabin as their own home, would think the piano house quite rich: even excessively rich, perhaps.

Now, the Tudor style of house was not something you typically saw in our western part of the country. Indeed, I had not seen a house like this one in a very long time. I think I saw something of its type a very long time ago and as far back east as I started out in life. This house was very likely the best example of its kind that I had ever seen.

Why I did not really notice the piano house until a piano played from inside it, I do not know. I suppose I was lost in my own walking to and fro, carrying my work. The sadness I also carried with me did likely also play a part in my own obliviousness.

I did not truly notice a good deal. I think I could say that I stared through most everything and everyone back then. I walked in a type of blindness or in a foggy state of being. The feelings of despairing aloneness can make you blind to the world around you.

Because I tended to keep so entirely to myself, I was never cognizant of who had lived in the piano house before the musician had come to live there, nor did I know a thing about whoever lived in that place of abode now. Since I was suddenly so very intrigued by the piano playing and especially that one song, I wished to know about the inhabitants of the piano house and became quite determined to become far more aware of any strangers in town than was usual for me. I could generally be called aloof. I kept to myself most times.

The structure itself was of a two story variety (though I do not include any attic above in this assessment). My mentions of the upper window would have intimated at least one upper floor. There were a generous amount of windows throughout the entire house I thought, and even in the upper floor where the magnificent music was created. I thought it a pretty house, though I was heavily influenced by the beautiful music emanating from it, and as I have said, I hadn't really noticed it before the piano played inside it.

Before I was drawn to the piano house, I had never thought twice about a Tudor style home. Although now, I do think, that if I could ever afford to have my own house built (or bought), I would want it in a Tudor piano house style like that one. I have become sentimental about that semblance of style for a structure of residence. It is the musician that has done that to me. That piano and especially its music have endeared me to the Tudor style of the piano house.

I could not say that I had walked past the piano house often prior to a piano playing from within it. In point of fact, I do not recall how many or few times I had ever passed by that house before the musician moved into it and began to play. Not daily, that is certain. But once I heard the music play, I could not resist going near it as often as could be reasonably done. As I have said,

I changed my route to include coming near to it. Any time I was required to go out relative to my work, I found my way to stroll beside the place where the musician lived. Indeed, with or without work related reasons for walking past, I now found excuses to take a daily walk. Yes, daily. I *had* to hear the music playing as often as could be done.

I will not say all now, for I prefer to save some certain details until a little later on, but, before the piano house called to me with its soul-penetrating music (at least the songs that pierced into my own spiritual being), I had only ever taken work home. I had never before accepted any work in anybody else's house. I did not wish to. I preferred to remain as independent as I possibly could; and I preferred to stay at home and work there as much as I was able. However, when the lady of the piano house asked me to come to work a little for her, I could not bring myself to refuse her proposal. I felt that I could not decline. Indeed, I was compelled to accept (but more on this hereafter).

It was a little later on that I walked inside that piano house. It was similar to what I had imagined, but it was a great deal different. The furnishings and the inner layout of the place were not quite exactly as I had pictured. I suppose I had simply and lazily tried to visually put my own place of lodging into that Tudor framework. I had not really thought a great deal about what it might in actuality be like inside that house. Some might think it a deal strange or my mind languid, that I had not endeavored to paint a proper picture of the piano house from the inside. Nonetheless, I simply had not done so.

I do admit that my mind had oftentimes wandered up the stairs, or more likely, up the outer Tudor wall that led into the window and into the room where the heavenly music was created. I was terribly curious to know what the musician looked like. I could not decide whether the musician was male or female. I could hardly begin to guess. I suppose I did not try to surmise that mystery for a good long time. That question and answer did not matter to me, at least not as yet.

THE MUSICIAN

Sometimes I wondered what the décor of that piano room was like. Was it luxurious or plainly utilitarian? Did the piano reside in a bedroom or an upper parlor of some kind? Was it such as a music room? Was it simply a small room with a piano and a few other instruments? Was it a small ballroom? Or, could it be an entire apartment suite that the piano and its player lived in? Did the piano player keep entirely to him or herself, something like a lodger? For the amount of time each day that the piano could be counted on to be playing, I could easily have guessed that the musician was little anywhere else, in the house or out of it.

I walked past that house enough times, at differing times of many different days, that I knew how much the musician had to have been playing. Many might call it an obsession. Some would call it a passion. Others might only call it simply practice. I trusted or at least hoped that no neighbors thought the seemingly constant music any annoyance to them. I could not really imagine such a thing. Surely the player's music edified and maybe even entertained all around the piano house?

The musician certainly had a penchant for fresh air. Even on the chilliest days, that upper window was most usually quite open. Outside air flowed in as the music flowed out. I sometimes wondered if the pianist felt any chill. Or, was he or she so deeply lost in their art that they could feel no coldness from without? I do know that I forgot feeling myself: for what the temperature might be around me, as I slowly walked by listening to the music, wholly engrossed by and lost in it.

When the musician was playing almost anything, and I was passing by, I did not ever wish to keep walking. I was surely prone to simply stand there. I came near to just simply leaning on the piano house fence many a time. I sometimes imagined a bench or at least a chair near the piano house, as near under that window as could be accomplished, where I could sit and listen. I would have closed my eyes and rested my weary soul from the worries and troubles of my life, even as I rested my feet.

11

3
On Errands

M any days of each week I walked a goodly piece. I picked up and brought work home to do, and then I would deliver the work back again. I took in laundry and mending, and other related odd jobs. I suppose you could say that I was the washer woman to many. I did not like to think of myself quite so lowly. I preferred to think of myself more of a needle worker, but I did have to wash, put out to dry, and iron a great number of articles of clothing and other such piecework, day in and day out.

I dared not say no to any honest work. I felt the need to earn my keep in a way. I wanted some coin to call my own and to do with as I wished. I believed in hiding some savings for some future day when I might need it. I did not want to feel any more beholding than I already did. I also wanted to know how to provide for me and mine should it ever become necessary to fully do so. Such a thing was not outside the realm of possibilities. I knew that I must be ready for anything. I did not want to leave myself open to destitution. I would not allow my family to starve or to be left outside in the cold without any shelter.

Mending and especially washing clothes was not a preferably chosen vocation for me, to be sure. It could be thoroughly exhausting work in differing ways, winter or summer. Extremes of cold and heat condemn their own unique cruelties. Nevertheless, there were always people who needed or wanted this sort of labor done and so I was thankful to be able to do it in exchange for money. I could hope for easier, better and more enjoyable employment some day, but, for now, I did not regret the occupation. I was very glad to be able to take such work home to do there. I did not wish to be away from home any more than need be. My time away, my work brought home, and the money that I made; it all seemed a valuable trade in my view.

The daily walking also did me good, I thought. Certain frustrations were dissolved and released through the beneficial exercise. Fresh air and sunshine were a boon to my heart. Many of the people I toiled for treated me kindly enough. However, if they did not, they could take their washing and mending elsewhere. I did not need to beg for work from those who would treat me cruelly. There was enough piecework of that laborious kind to do, that I could pick and choose my customers (or employers) to a good degree.

I knew that many wondered why I took on such a lowly trade to begin with. An outsider's view of my circumstances might be that I was not and never would be destitute. Many did not know the entire truth about me and what I lived with. There were those who were likely suspicious of what I was forced to live under, perhaps, but most did not have an inkling of my true life.

I did not speak to anyone of my daily realities. I preferred to show a happy front. I only shared my smiling face. I did not let out my aching heart to any person. My hell was a purely private one. I was not at liberty to share my current life's burdens with one living soul on earth.

Yes, the matron of my house did see and hear some of what went on. Still, she lived in her own reality because of her own particular seat at the family table. She did not want to admit to herself the full truth that played out before her and behind walls near her. I could not speak with her about so many things. It was not possible. It was the situation, you see. Well, I suppose you do not see as yet, dear reader. However, I will tell you by and by; and then, you will come to understand of what I now evasively but painfully hint at.

And so, day by day, week upon week, I washed and hung to dry, the clothing that I then ironed and sometimes mended before taking back to their owners to wear again. All this was more toil than I preferred. I would have wished to sew more and wash less. I would have liked to limit myself to needlework. I enjoyed creating clothing with needle and thread. I enjoyed the new fabrics. I didn't even mind the fittings with the ladies. We would talk as I worked. Light talk, diverting chatter: such distractions as this helped me to forget my troubles. Anything to dim or wash away my sorrows, even for a short time, was a very good thing.

But, it was the washing of dirty laundry that the ladies typically wanted done by me. Can you believe that I would sometimes pray for even a little mending to vary and especially lighten my load of work? Yes, I hoped and prayed for even a little mending rather than all the washing, which always included the hanging to dry and the ironing. Rain or snow, heat or cold, laundry was a painful drudgery in its way.

Now and then I would fervently pray that more sewing jobs would come my way from ladies in and around the town. Though, it was mostly not to be, at least for the time being. The womenfolk generally preferred to send away for their dresses oftentimes, if they could afford it. From the east, or from England and maybe even a few dresses were sent for from Paris. I did not really know where the fashionable dresses originally came from. I did not pay great attention to such stylish things. I dressed quite humbly myself, at least compared to those for whom I worked; and anything beyond the plain, simple or practical, was not on my own mind, especially for myself.

Some women who were financially living in-between, being unable to afford to send away for fancy ready-made dresses, and yet not so poor that they must sew their own simple dresses for themselves; would sometimes hire me to act as their own seamstress. I came more cheaply than dresses from eastward, and having me sew was easier than sewing for themselves, of course. I was happy to help in that way. It was a help to a lady and a help to myself. And, as you can well imagine, new needlework was far more pleasant than washing the dirty clothing of other folks or even the mending of their older things.

When the matron of the piano house sent for me to interview with her, I fully intended to accept almost any honest proposal of employment from her. I did not entertain the thought of working there for easier work. I did not actually care if she only wished for me to do her washing for her. I did not even hope a moment for more pleasant labors. I desired to at least step inside the house where the beautiful music played, for a time, any time, as often as may be accomplished and within the bounds of my own household limitations.

When I first went to work for the lady of the piano house, the work was as heavy as I had assumed it might be. Washing of clothing and even deep cleaning round about inside that house were my first assignments. Gradually, though, she entrusted easier chores to my capable hands. Soon I was doing a little mending and even other very light work for her. Still, when the musician played, no matter what the labor required of me, the work seemed light indeed. As fingers flew over the piano upstairs, the time for me, flew too. However, this work inside the musician's house came to me a little later.

4
Rumors

As I went about gathering and delivering my work by day, certain unsolicited hearsay was given to me from time to time by various folks, and I began to hear rumors about the eccentrically reclusive person that many besides me often wondered about. Whether or not I had asked a thing at all about the mysterious musician in the piano house, I was frequently told of what people knew, thought they knew, and what they had imagined.

There was growing interest in the puzzling person of unknown name who stayed and played upstairs in that house of music. This musician had unwittingly instigated lively speculation in our town. Curiosity about the pianist seemed continual. Questions abounded.

Why did the musician hide upstairs soulfully playing piano, violin and other instruments for hours on end? Was the musical player a man or a woman, younger or older, crazy or sane? Why was the identity of pianist kept as such a secret? How was the musician related to the cautious lady and gentleman who were new inhabitants of that house? Why were that older couple so very guarded about the secluded person who played throughout days and even into the nights? Was the musician their son or their daughter, or somebody else entirely? Why were servants of the house generally kept from that particular piano room or even the entire set of apartment rooms upstairs?

The musician had never been seen by anyone that I knew of. Some of the day servants had said that the piano player was entirely kept hidden from them. The man and lady of the house took care of every personal request of the musician. In a little world alone with musical instruments, this cloistered person seemed so unnaturally shy to all those folks who were normally not.

The workers of that house had near nothing to tell, for they knew no details of import. They knew next to nothing about he or she who played. They generally assumed and speculated, about as much as the rest of the townspeople.

Apparently, trays of food and drink were brought to the piano room door, or at least to a door of the upstairs set of rooms. Emptied trays were taken away later. Pitchers of water were taken to and from as well. Water was heated for bathing. Towels and some laundry went to and fro. I had thought that the personal laundry could tell the tale of the musician, such as the clothing of a man or a woman. However, apparently the lady of the house took care to mix all things of that telling nature in with everything else herself. Who knew what items were hers, her husband's or belonging to the mystery person who hid in the rooms upstairs: nobody beyond those who were a part of the secret themselves.

The musician was never seen because this peculiar person did not wish to be seen. The piano player did not want to see or speak to anyone. Such a fact was quite obvious. Only the lady and lord of the manor ever spoke with the musician. No other living being was ever allowed to even attempt such a thing.

Contact with the reticent person was considered formally forbidden, though as if in an unwritten way. The musician was not spoken of at all, as if not even in existence. The musical instrument player was a non-subject in that house.

Some assumptions about the secretive pianist were reasonable but many rumors absolutely ran wild. Rampant and wide ranging were the ideas about the musician. Was this musical player akin to a hideous hunchback or a lunatic genius? Hearsay of that silly sort was quite common in and around town.

Yes, many of our townsfolk did indeed discuss at length such things as, 'he was possibly a severe hunchback' or, 'she is a dreadful lunatic'. Some people thought that maybe he was extremely rotund and eccentrically secretive of that fact, though there was absolutely no evidence of copious eating in that upstairs apartment. To the contrary, actually: little food seemed taken and eaten in general.

Speculations ran on like a rolling stream... 'He must be hideous beyond belief to hide away like that. Perhaps she was terribly scarred beyond recognition of former beauty, for some tragic and horrific reason. Was he a musical genius madman playing and scribbling away at musical compositions? Was she so very broken-hearted from a lost love as to hide herself away from the world to play piano alone forevermore?'

What was the secret story behind this cloistered life that seemed barely lived, up in that set of rooms in that melodious house? Who was the musician and why was such a solitary existence chosen by him or her? And why did the two known residents of the house remain so excessively hushed about their strangely secluded lodger? What true secrets had they each to hide from the town in particular and maybe the world at large? Why had they moved way out here amongst us to hide their musician away from our town? Why were they now hiding out west? Who might they be hiding from?

As townsfolk generally fixated upon the oddly secretive family, I focused more on the numerous harmonious melodies flowing out the window and into my heart. One hauntingly beautiful song in particular had captured my mind. I wondered on questions other than what the musician looked like and even why she or he was hiding and playing. Would I ever meet the musician? Could I someday thank this seeming kindred spirit for pulling me out of my fog of desolation, and renewing some of my faith and hopes once more? I would never be the same again. I had heard the music playing. Yes, I had already changed.

As for myself and my speculations, based on my own somewhat recent experiences of life, I tended more towards thinking that this isolated soul was mostly lost in sorrows. Perhaps the dweller of some upstairs rooms of that piano house was cosseting their heart for a time, in a way of healing it. I had heard the music enough to know or at least to believe that there was great injury of spirit, and also passion there. The musical airs that emanated out of that particular upper window spoke to me in a way that I thought I deeply understood.

The music almost cried in and of itself sometimes. My heart ached for that musician. My soul was drawn to the piano player. I interpreted the confinement as possibly a temporary thing: a type of grieving, perhaps. I guessed that the inhabitant of those upper rooms of the piano house needed societal protection for a time. Maybe the resident was in mourning. The music felt that way to me.

I did not share my inward suspicions or guesses with anyone as added hearsay. I only listened to what came my way. I never really sought out the gossip that floated around the town. I cannot say, however, that I was not curious enough to listen to what was voluntarily told to me. I could not help but listen and wonder. I did not like to hear the wildest rumors that I found to be unbelievable nonsense, though I could not help paying attention to any facts that might shed some light on the truth of the situation in that household. Who could *not* be interested, at least a little?

When Mrs. Weiss (for that was the name of the lady of the piano house) asked me in to interview to work for her, I made a conscious decision not to pry for any information that was not desired to be freely given. Over a little time, I think that in a way, Mrs. Weiss began to trust me, and so entrust me with easier work sooner, because she sensed that I was not a common gossip. This kind of thing was obviously important to her. She did not desire any tattlers working for her and within her walls. Of course she did not wish to invite busy-bodies under her roof.

Mrs. Weiss made no mentions to me of any gossip going around when I began to work for her. If she knew of any of the speculations about the pianist residing upstairs, she did not allude to as much. As far as I could tell by anything she said to me, she did not have any idea that people talked about her musician. Though of course I surmised, and likely correctly, that Mrs. Weiss must surely know that the townsfolk were buzzing with open and verbal curiosity about he or she who played up the stairs in her home.

While I was there in the piano house working for Mrs. Weiss, there was the occasional thing said relative to the musician by this or that other person who worked there. It did not take much for any person to be dismissed. To appear nosy was not acceptable. Thus I saw why I was called for, to interview for work there; and so I imagined that I was given more in the way of trusted or easy work. Any person working within those walls who did not display their trustworthiness, was soon gone, or sent packing, you could say. The lady of piano manor did not want a sort of spy in her midst.

One conversation early on leant a little hint to me. In fact, I seem to recall this the first time I talked with Mrs. Weiss.

She had said to me, "I understand that you are a bit of a solitary soul, Isabelle."

I answered, "Yes, I suppose that you could say that about me, Mrs. Weiss."

"You keep to yourself."

"Yes, I think that I do."

"I understand the solitary kind, Isabelle."

I did not wish to say 'yes' to allude to the person upstairs and so I simply uttered, "I have always been a little reserved, Mrs. Weiss."

"You are a shy sort."

"Yes."

"You don't care to join in on all the idle gossip of the town."

"No."

"I like that about you, Isabelle. I initially had heard hinted as much and then I could see that about you right away. I have no use for silly women who engage in idle chit-chat."

I innocently agreed, "I understand what you are saying, Mrs. Weiss."

She instantly seemed more than just a shade agitated, "You *understand*? *What* do you understand?"

21

I feared that I had caused her to misunderstand me relative to knowing or suspecting something more than she had wished me to, and so I tried to rectify, "Well, there are those who wish to spend their time on *better* things, I would say."

"Oh, yes. Right you are, Isabelle. If only more people would mind to their *own* affairs, like I do believe that you tend towards."

"Oh dear, I am far too exhaustedly busy to place my energies beyond my own work and family."

"Yes, exactly."

5
New Work

I suppose Mrs. Weiss heard of me and my honest work from a neighbor or a friend, perhaps somebody at church, or maybe more likely from someone for whom I had done work. As I have mentioned already, I could not resist going to her proposed interview. I wanted to walk into that house. I hoped to hear the music playing from inside the house at least once. I wished that I could hear my song on that piano from a closer vantage point of hearing. Would I be privy to harmonious notes on the inside of the piano house that could not be heard from outside it? I certainly thought as much. Since the sounds of lower notes do seem to me to travel farther than higher notes, I fully expected to be treated to some musical details that range higher on the piano scale.

Of course I was curious to see or meet the musician. I felt a desire to thank that pianist. Still, in a sense, from another part within me, I did *not* wish to meet the musician. It is difficult to explain why I would not want to meet and speak to the player of that beautiful song that had become as if my own, but I had a few reasons to feel that way.

Perhaps part of it was that I feared if I met the music maker, the ethereal mystique of the song might dissipate into the ether to a degree. I did not want that song to lose any of its value to me. What if I did not like the musician as a person? No, it was not that I would dislike the song if the player were unattractive in some way. If the wild gossip was somehow true that the musician was a hideous hunchback or a shockingly scarred young lady, that kind

of outward thing would not matter to me one jot. If it turned out
to be true that the pianist was in some way ugly, I would care about
that person all the more, I should say. The beauty was in the music
and came from the soul. The body did not matter. The outward
appearance of the musician was of no account to me. I was turned
and attuned to the heart.

No, it was other less wild imaginings or speculations that
came into my mind. What if I became at odds with the musician
for some reason? What if he or she was not a kind or good
person? What if the piano player was somehow harsh and cruel
to me? Passionate people can be that way sometimes, I surmised.
If something happened to put me at odds with the musician
personally, all the magic of hearing that song might evaporate. I did
not wish the supernal power of that main melody to be diminished
in any way. I could not risk losing that song of mine now that I had
found it.

I wanted to leave things be, just as they were. I hoped that
all could stay the same, at least for now. I needed that song. I
desperately wanted to keep it close to me. And so, no, I did not
truly want to meet the musician. I only wanted to hear the music
from inside the house for a change and closer enjoyment.

Unlike some homes of this larger size, no servants were kept
at all times. None lived in the house. Not even one all-work maid.
Such strangers were not wanted within the piano house every
waking and sleeping hour. I wondered if the musician sometimes
milled about the rest of the house once any servants were gone
home each night. I suspected as much. 'Why not?', I thought.

A few of the household helpers worked at the piano house
daily, putting in many hours for Mrs. Weiss most days of each
week. I, however, did not agree to such work. I only came a few
afternoons each week at most, or maybe much of a day here or
there. I had other responsibilities. I could not commit to such
overarching employment. A little of almost each day is one thing.
A greater portion of every day is another. I could not be gone
from my own home so very much. I supposed that Mrs. Weiss was

satisfied to take what she could get from me.

It was more important to Mrs. Weiss to have discreet workers who gave her honest labors for the money that she paid, than to simply have anyone else putting in time there at her home. She wanted to know that she could trust the employees within her walls. I certainly could understand that way of thinking and doing. Even without a secretive musician hiding upstairs, would not most folks prefer trusted workers in their home?

At first, it was laborious laundry for me. I sighed to know that more drudgery would be mine, but, once there, and once the piano was playing, the time melted away. The work was not work. It was almost as if my spirit was transported out of my body to float high in the sky, listening. My ears would rule those moments. My soul would inhabit my musical mind and sentimental heart as, in an almost truly real way, my body trudged along without me.

My hands worked, but I was not as if working. My arms moved, but I was barely aware of the work that I was doing. Sweat could blanket my brow and further, but I did not feel the heat or my own exertions. I was one with the music. My laboring body was somewhere else. I suppose one could say that my soul flew skyward while my body worked on earth.

If the musical portion was happy, I felt the joy it leant to me. If the music evoked sadness, I sorrowed with the player, and also for myself. I shared burdens or delights with the musician. My inner heart sang and it cried, as the music dictated. I was as if a sort of slave to that master. What masterful power a musician can exercise over his or her hearers. Whatever I might be feeling before the piano, violin or other insturment began to play, my command of my own mood was overthrown by the notes and how they were executed.

Sometimes loud and sometimes soft: the musician's fingers would oftentimes either glide across or pound upon those piano keys. When the music was played delicately, I worked more slowly and as quietly as may be accomplished, trying to hear every note, for I did not wish to miss a single one. When thunderous, I needed not strain to take in every bit of it. I preferred the musician to play fairly loudly. I wished to hear the songs, the individual notes, and the overall intensity: the musical magic.

No matter how instinctively pulled from me, applause was not permitted, of course. This was not a spoken or written law of Mrs. Weiss, but simply an obvious fact to me. There could not be any 'bravo' sent up towards the musician. Of course, like all who worked in the piano house, I understood that I was supposed to be pretending that there was no music playing at all. How could I possibly break into grateful clapping when any beautiful song was completed to my satisfaction? I could not. Sometimes it took quite an effort on my part to remember that I must not show in the least degree how greatly I appreciated the music that swelled in the house of the piano.

Since any compliment to the musician must wait for who knew how long, if not for forever, I chose to save my words of praise and gratitude until that day might come. It was that, or never. How could I possibly do otherwise anyhow? And, in the meantime, I continued to thank the Heavens in prayer for the music that blessed me in this way.

So the intermittent days passed by: I diligently did my work for Mrs. Weiss, and she was content with my efforts. My hands labored as my mind was engaged blissfully or at least intently elsewhere. My heart or spirit was upstairs near the piano in its way.

Then one day, when one of the lighter work maids was caught in a clandestine whisper about the mystery of the musician, she was dismissed, and I was promoted. I was doomed to laundry drudgery and such toil no more. My reddened and sometimes near raw hands were given rest. There was a little mending and sewing for me to do, a little dusting, and simply general attending to Mrs. Weiss and whatever little thing that she might want or need done by me. At worst, I was now a light work maid; but in some ways, on some days, I was as if a lady's maid. I liked this idea a good deal.

There was light conversation. There was listening. I mostly listened to Mrs. Weiss, often as I sewed something up for her. She had a penchant for point-work and other fine needlework and was delighted to find that I had quite a talent or at least some skill for such work. She began to think of little projects she fancied for me to create for her. I was quite delighted to be given such easy and pleasantly creative work. I was even allowed by her to take some of that kind of work home with me, and I was in effect, paid quite generously for every hour of work. Yes, it was becoming quite a handsome job for me.

The only shortcoming of my new position in my view was that I could not so often drift away in my head while my ears drank in the musician's songs. When Mrs. Weiss was talking, I was forced to turn my mind to her words instead of the songs that were almost always playing upstairs. I could not appear rude. I could not show any listlessness in regard to her conversation. I knew that I must pay attention to her; for that was in a good part what she paid me to do.

Once I was allowed to take some of the needlework home that Mrs. Weiss paid me to do for her, I was able to say no to some other work, and was also able to work more hours in the piano house. In point of fact, this was specifically discussed and arranged by Mrs. Weiss with me.

One day she simply said, "How can I keep you with me *more*, Isabelle? I want you working here in my house more hours and days, or at least more often."

"I am very sorry, but I cannot be away from my home too very much, Mrs. Weiss."

"But, you can take work home to make up that difference, and I am willing to pay *more* for each and every hour and task. Can you not let some of your other work go? I want you to myself, I think. Can you become my own exclusive helper, Isabelle?"

I thought a moment and offered, "Well, I suppose if I am only or at least *mostly* only working for you, I could work here more, as long as I could take some of the work home. I still must have that. You see, I must put my family first. I have never worked so much away from home before."

"I will give you leeway. I will make it worth your while. I won't ask you to sacrifice your family on *my* account. I understand your priorities. I am more flexible on that count than you might imagine."

And so we struck a bargain. I would generally decline work for other folks so that I might concentrate my efforts on behalf of Mrs. Weiss, while never neglecting my own home and family preeminent obligations. If I was needed at home, Mrs. Weiss was patient with me. She had come to trust me and she did not wish to unduly burden me. I was more happily employed than ever. My family was not encumbered nor neglected. I made more money. The work was light. My employer was flexible. And the musician played upstairs.

6
Singing Lullabies

It had been a while since I had sung lullabies to my beloved children. As I was tucking my dear little ones into their bed one night, I was mightily trying to remember the completeness of that effulgent song, my topmost favorite amongst the musician's offerings, humming its tune partially in my head and then aloud. In my meager attempt, I was painfully reminded that my babies were not being sung to every night as I had once done for them. Suddenly, those days of nightly lullabies seemed far too long ago.

Once upon a more hopeful time, I had always thought that I would sing to my children every night to help guide them to their slumbers: at least while they were still little ones. I long thought that I would sing them their lullabies nightly until they were old enough to beg me to stop. I wished to sing them to sleep until they were too old to need it anymore; but, there had been too many nights along the way that I had felt so terribly low of soul that I could not sing without crying.

Sometimes I *did* cry as I sang my children to sleep. In the dark, they did not see my tears, and they were still fully young enough not to notice my sniffles or my wavering voice. Every time I sang to my young ones, I attempted my best not to fall into weeping, especially as deep as towards sobbing. They did sometimes notice that kind of crying and always wished to know why I was so forlorn. What had hurt me? I could not tell them. Indeed, there was not a single soul on earth that I could tell of my deep aching. I was left with my own pain. I was alone with my sorrows.

Yes, dear reader, as some might counsel me, I had tried to turn to prayers for comfort, and indeed, I do think that sometimes I did find a certain level of solace through my praying; but, there were times when the comfort did not seem to come at all, and my aloneness deepened to think that Heaven did not care for my aching heart. Was there no angel or spirit, or single soul in Heaven who cared for or about me? Would my intense loneliness and sorrows carry on with me into the eternities? I too oftentimes thought as much.

It is true that when I had been blessed with my children, I was comforted at least by them. I found my only joy in life because of and with them. If I focused on my children, all else could melt away. All my regrets could vanish, at least for a time; when I thought of, attended to or held my children. When I was only their mother, my world was complete in its way. My youthful hopes and dreams could be forgotten for a time.

The first songs I had ever sung to my first baby, my daughter Lorna, were pulled from my memory of any song that my mother had ever sung to me, and then from any childhood songs I could recall. I had always especially enjoyed singing Christmas carols. By the time my son Alan was born, I had a full customary repertoire of lullabies, childhood songs and hymns from church-going as well. Nevertheless, somewhere along the way, I had stopped singing lullabies for my children.

And so, on that particular night, my attempts at humming the musician's song, which had for some time become my own, turned to my wanting to hum for my children once again. I chose to remember other songs instead. I began to hum and then sing one lullaby or other familiar song after another, that I had so many times shared with my children before. In a way miraculous to me, my tears did not emerge. Sadness did not overwhelm me as too oftentimes before.

Tiny Alan looked up at me with a very curious stare, "Mommy? Why are you singing like that?"

I felt shamefully horrid. Had it been that terribly long since I had sung a lullaby to my babies? Had my small lad forgotten those days of songs and nights of lullabies?

Little Lorna echoed my thoughts somewhat when she reminded her brother, though with an almost scolding voice, "Silly Alan. Don't you remember how Mommy always used to sing to us? Don't you remember her nighttime songs to help us go to sleep?"

Alan matter-of-factly clarified, "Yes, but she always used to blow out the candle first I think. Or did she blow out a lamp first?"

Lorna filled in her little brother's line of thinking, "Yes, you are right, Alan. Mommy usually saved most of her singing to us, for in the darkness. You still see a light."

I thought I would help out, "Yes, my little dears, I often blew out either the lamp or the candle first, before I began singing my lullabies for you."

I feared to dare mention and remind how I used to sing to them in daytime too. I felt the guilt of having been an absent mother, a little because of my work away, but so much more because I had lost the desire to sing and thus had stopped altogether for such a lengthy time. I determined to do better again. The musician's songs had gradually reminded me of the power of music to lift one's soul, and I could not forget to enlist such joyful edification in my children's lives. I would do my best to feel up to singing lullabies to my children every night like I once used to do. I would try to sing to them more in the daytime. Indeed, I thought it long overdue that I should get them singing with me. I knew that it was long since high time that I taught them to sing some songs.

Since there is often no time quite like the present moment, I asked my little children to sing a little song with me. I picked an easy one and taught them the accompanying words. I thought that they might already know the tune, at least deep down or back in their minds, since I had sung it many times that long while ago. Thus, there in the flickering candle light, we sang the simple song together. Their bright faces shone out with joy as they mimicked the melody a little and fumbled the words a good deal.

When I was quite obviously about to blow out their candle

flame, with thoughts to soon leave them to their slumbers, Alan asked, "Another one? I want another one."

Lorna agreed, "Yes, might we try another, Mommy?"

They suddenly chimed sweetly together, "Please?"

How could I not? Of course I must. And so it was another little song that they tried to sing with me, each of us invariably laughing as we went. But then the night was nigh unto late now, and so I gently insisted that it was time for them to sleep, and for me to go prepare to do likewise.

Lorna begged, "Just one more song, Mommy?"

Alan added, "Can you sing us one little lullaby?"

Lorna entreated, "Only just one lullaby before you go?"

Alan directed, "Blow out the light first, like you used to do."

I blew out the candle flame. I chose an old favorite tune of mine. I sang the lullaby. I repeated it a number of times, softer and quieter each time, until their little eyes seemed firmly closed from what I could see in the bedroom moon and starlit darkness. I kissed their sweet small foreheads. I wiped salty drops from my cheeks. I left my almost sleeping children, to prepare to sleep for the night myself.

But first, I thought myself a little prayer of thanks to God for sending me the musician who had reminded me of the power of songs. I would not forget to sing for and with my dear children ever again. I promised myself that night, and I made a promise to Heaven too. I could not forget to mother my children rightly, no matter what ached in my own heart. They deserved no less, and indeed they had a right to so much more.

7
Looking Back

In my budding youth I was naïve, hopeful, trusting, loving, giving and buoyantly happy. I could seem to only imagine good. And though my parents were not to credit for all this, because they were not generally protective and nurturing; still, I was somehow naturally able to believe in better things. I had hope for my own future life. I did not doubt that I would marry and be happy. As 'Little Miss Barrett' (that which some called me), I was full of trusting effervescence; and how could I imagine at that time in my blossoming youthfulness, that I would look on life any differently later on?

Somehow I always knew that I could love any good man who treated me rightly. If I was loved, I would love in kind. When I was young, much younger, I thought that a man for me should be reasonably attractive at least, but my expectations and needs were not ever especially high in that regard. I did not wish to end up loving an ugly man, but as I grew a little older, I knew that if it came to it, I would rather love and marry a homely fellow who was honest and kind, over a dashingly handsome man who mistreated me in any way. What good is a beautiful face if you cannot trust the words coming out of the mouth? What good is a strongly masculine attractive form, if the manly hands are inclined to hit you?

In growing up, I did not think anything odd or terribly imperfect about my parents and family. I suppose I thought what I lived with as quite normal. What else did I truly know? It was when I left home as a young married woman and lived a while amongst other people, that I began to look back on my childhood and could see especially my parents in a differing light. In the illumination of comparisons, I could see things that had been wrong with them, and with our family.

When I was with child that first time, I thought at length about what kind of mother I wanted to be. I deeply desired to do better than my own mother had done with me. I wanted my husband to be a better father. I did not wish to harbor any ill will towards my parents for their mistakes, you understand: I only wanted *not* to repeat their mistakes and sins (of commission and omission) against their children, and to do far better than they had done with my own earthly-sent angels. I wanted to do my very best, always.

When my parents happily hurried me into marrying my husband, the young and dashing Mr. Ramstock, I thought nothing wrong with this. He was more handsome than I needed or expected. He was charming. I had full expectations of him being a good husband to me. I tended to think that if I was the best wife to him that I could be, he could not but also treat me well. Of course he would appreciate me in my every attempt at goodness, would he not? This idea seemed an eternal equation that could not fail to add up to perfect happiness. Good upon good should equal nothing less than good, I did think and fully believe at that time.

Indeed, I had spent a good portion of my flowering into womanhood years working at becoming the kind of wife that a good husband would want and even treasure. I practiced to be the kind of wife that most any man could not help but adore. Back at that time, I thought that to garner the love of a husband, all a wife need do was to shine in every womanly way that she could.

I had made myself a good cook. I could bake many wonderful things. I sewed and mended. I knew how to get a house clean, and quickly too. I was good with children, and I tended to love them each and all as well. I could milk a cow and tend to a garden, I could chop wood and even build things, and do other chores that men generally kept as their own. I wanted to be ready for anything. I was prepared to accept and help even a poor man. I wished to be a perfect helpmeet. I wanted to please any man who should end up as my husband. I sang and I played piano quite well I thought. I knew many songs. I could draw or paint a likeness pretty nicely. I knew many popular dances and older ones as well. I had worked hard to become as good a prospective wife as I could possibly do.

While still quite in my youth, I seemed to myself to be quite the eligible little woman. As young Miss Isabelle Barrett, I thought that my prospects for a good and happy husband very bright indeed. I had readied myself to please my man and I fully expected that when I married, my husband would please me as well. Why should he not? When he saw what a good wife he had caught, why should he not wish to please me as well? Indeed! Everything added up to perfect happiness, I believed.

How had I met and caught my husband you might wonder? My parents had simply arranged the match. They had met him through someone they knew, his eyes had caught on me, and they had decided that he was to be for me. I was married to him before I knew it. I must say that I wanted to be out of their house as much as they wanted me off of their hands, and so I was entirely pliable in the matter. I confess I as much married to escape them as to forge into a new life of my own making. With my husband everything charming at first, and my parents long cold and cruel, why would I not?

There was a group of travelers going further to points west which my new husband and I would join up with, and so my ma and pa were rid of me for good, and me of them, because there was no turning back once I went fully west. I did not truly think myself ill treated, for I thought that my handsome fellow of a husband loved me, and so I easily loved him in return. I fully believed that I would build a happy life with him. I had always sensed that I could love if I were loved and well treated, as I have said before. I had not known much of that kind of adulthood reality, but I could certainly imagine it.

When I was first married to become Mrs. Isabelle Ramstock, I thought that my husband loved me well enough, as I have stated.

I did not fear that I could coax him into loving me all the more, day to day, even as I was a good wife to him. When he did not rise to stand up on the pedestal I had set up for him, I still had all the hope and faith that he would someday do so. Soon, I thought. Not too far off, I hoped.

I did not despair as I suffered one little disappointment after another. I persisted. I trudged forward. I endured. When I was first with child, I thought that, '*now* my husband would love me as he should'. Now he would thank the Heavens for his dear wife who was going to suffer through travail to give him this precious gift of life. He wanted a son. I hoped to give him his heart's desire. In my own heart, I hoped he would grow to love me more than he had heretofore done, for our child that we would share together, *whether* son or daughter.

As I grew in size and discomfort, my husband's neglect, mistreatment and abandonment grew. I did not as yet lose much hope. I held out near a full faith. I looked forward to the day that he would hold our child in his arms and would then deeply love both our baby and its mother. I pictured his change. I imagined all things better than they were. I believed that my giving him our baby would change him for the better.

And when I felt the indescribably profound love for my first Heaven-sent child, I seemed to think that my husband shared that love for our baby. I simply assumed that my feelings were his feelings. I thought that as my love for my husband had deepened because of our having a darling baby together, that he would or even that he *did* already love me more as well.

It was not so. Nothing had changed. He had not changed, at least not for the better, and particularly towards me. He did not seem to love me or our baby much at all. I explained all this disappointment away to myself and naïvely hoped forward once more. I excused my husband's stubborn coldness because I had not given him his wished-for son. I told myself that perhaps this daughter was for me and that soon I would please my husband with our son. Little Lorna was not the baby he had expected. She was not a boy.

Once our son Alan was finally born, I thought I noticed a proud happiness there in my husband's demeanor and visage. He seemed to love his *boy*, at least. There was a kind of sentimental happiness, it seemed to me. I hoped it would grow into something of more value over time. I tried to picture our son growing up and gradually becoming the light of my husband's life. I could be happy with *that* at least, I surmised. I did still hope that whatever was wrong in my husband's heart would heal from this somewhat sad beginning.

As some years passed, my unfounded hopes faded into my unhappy reality. My husband was gone more and more. At first I was frustrated and inwardly complained to myself that he wished to leave his little family. Then, as continual cruelties wore my spirit down, I learned to dread when he came home at all. I came to cherish his time away from us and I went so very far as to thank the Heavens above that the father of my children was gone as much as he was, and yes, dear reader, I fear to admit, even to pray that he might never return.

My husband was charming enough before I married him. How could I imagine prior to becoming his wife that he would change into something entirely different? Was he completely deceitful in his efforts to catch me in marriage? I had been honest with him in everything, and so I therefore assumed that the faithful and kind man that he presented himself before me was his true self. However, I was to be betrayed. He was not who he had seemed to be. Perhaps I had been blind to the real man before me, right from the beginning. Maybe I saw who I wished to see in the first place.

As I gradually came to see my husband clearly, my devastation was also gradual, though profound. When I saw that he would rather feign love in flirtations or worse with any other woman, than to work at attempts to truly love his own wife, my heart was broken beyond measure. I cried out foul at him many a time and then as he angrily struck blow upon blow against me, the pains of those assaults wracked my body and shocked my soul. After I felt the sinking realities attending injury after injury, I became deadened to everything, within and without.

In a lengthy fog of some sort of suddenness, as I became a wife; the horrible nightmare of my new life killed the young lady that I had been. I was left a stranger to myself. No longer did I know who I was. I was a shell of a being. I did not know who to *be* anymore. I could not go back to the young and innocent girl that I was before. I could not go home. There was nowhere I could go to escape my new misery of life. It was a near death.

When my first child was born, I found happiness in that little person. My little Lorna was my life that relatively short time before another child came into being. I fairly quickly had another baby, and so little Lorna and tiny Alan were my only living world. My one joy in life was in those two little ones. I could not find any happiness with the man that I was yoked to. He was my burden. He was my hellish nightmare.

Looking honestly back on it, I suppose I could admit that my husband did surely seem to love me at first. Perhaps only for those initial few weeks or maybe even as much as two months, but then whatever love he might have held for me faded away terribly quickly. I have since heard it said by some that men are not inclined or designed to love one woman for longer than the initial honeymooning period of a marriage: that when that earliest flame bursts forth, it is a fire that roars for a little time and then dies down, even to die altogether into cooling and then spent coals. I could not ever generally believe such a horrid thing for women-kind (and even mankind), but I do confess that there have been times that I feared that this might be generally so.

Is this theory a truth? I truly hope not. Such a brief devotional interest is worldly or of animal nature perhaps, but not of the divine, Heavenly or eternal. I grant you, dear reader, that even the truest love sparks brightly in the beginning and will settle down into embers, but is there not such a thing as a true love that forever burns warmly, if not always white hot, between a man and his woman? I hold to this belief. I have my ideals. I have seen enough married couples to hold to a little faith on this subject. There are many men and women in marriage who seem truly happily in love after many years together.

No, I do sense that true love in marriage all does generally come down to choosing to hold to one's vows or not. When a man and his woman work together in their marriage, their marriage should work *for* them, to keep them happily together. I know what I am able to offer, have given or at least *was* willing to give. Why could I not have found and married a man of my own who would have given as much to me as I would to him? I could have then been happy in marriage. But, alas, that was not to be for me. My husband chose to live otherwise. He chose to take, instead of to give.

And as to my own reality, or where and how I live now, we finally moved to live with my husband's mother (or with his parents, I should say) and it was not long at all before I was quite glad to have done it. I ate far better. I worked less hard. The house was large enough to offer me buffered space from my husband. My father-in-law aside, my mother-in-law was most always home. My husband was forced to mind his manners better in his mother's house. He could not hit me openly for she was around us to notice and might not like to see such a thing.

I confess that my husband and I both watched our words better too. There was a certain and solid pretense of peace and harmony to be kept up to a degree. We were both feigning a decent sort of marriage. A general almost politeness permeated between my husband and me, when his mother's ears were anywhere near.

Mrs. Ramstock was at least a kindly woman. She loved my children and that was enough for me. That was a certain boon I might not have expected. She was a fully pleasant surprise. I had not dared to hope for a pleasant mother-in-law. Indeed, I had feared worse than unpleasantness. Based on my experiences with the son, why should I have expected a kindly mother-in-law? I had not hoped for so good a woman. I truly appreciated that she treated me well and adored my children, as their grandmother.

My husband's mother, in her goodly way, almost made up for her ungodly son.

8
All Quiet

I had been away from the Weiss home for at least a week. My children had been quite sick and I simply would not try to bring myself to leave them only to their grandmother's care until they were entirely on the mend. They must be happy and healthy or I would not leave them. I could not go out to work. I must stay home and tend to my children's needs until they were sick no more. I had sent word to Mrs. Weiss and she had graciously sent patient words back to me. She could certainly wait for my return until my children were completely well again.

Once my children were back to their generally healthy selves, I finally walked my way back to work for Mrs. Weiss. As I gradually neared the Weiss home, that one fine clear day, I noticed an unusual silence. All was quiet. At least the air seemed far more quiet than usual. It was a strange hush. I could hear certain noises in the distance and round about, but something was missing. I had not been used to this seeming stillness in the air. The music was missing. The musician was not playing.

The songs of birds, the sounds of people and all other usual noises that had once been typical around here before the musician came to live in our town (though still not quite amongst us), seemed a sort of silence now. I suddenly realized that it had been a very long time since I had walked to, from or near the Weiss home when the musician was not playing. It all felt so very strange. It felt sad to me. The piano was silent. There was no violin. No instrument played. I was sad that the piano was quiet. Though, I trusted that it would play again soon. Any moment, I believed. The musician must surely play again before too very long.

From the moment that I had become cognizant of the entire lack of music emanating from the piano window, to the many minutes after I had finally entered into the Weiss home, I was waiting, and almost with bated breath. I waited for the music to begin again. As Mrs. Weis asked me about how my children now were feeling, and I told her that they were quite well again, I was still waiting for the musician to begin to play once more. Throughout my stitching for my employer and my quiet conversations with her, I waited for the music. Yet, the piano house remained eerily silent and still.

Those two hours that I was there working my first day back (since my children had been ill), the silence unnerved me. What was wrong with the musician? Was he or she sick? Was he or she too deeply depressed to care about his or her music? I wondered why the musician did not play today. As those two hours turned into two days of me coming there and then more, I wondered still more. I did not catch the musician playing at all. Not one single note. Not a sound.

Perhaps there had been music when I was not there, but that seemed unlikely to me. It would be quite a strange coincidence if there was music only when I was out of the range of hearing it. No, I thought that there was something definitely and perhaps terribly wrong. The music had stopped and I could not ask Mrs. Weiss why. My wondering over this mystery was near driving me mad.

Each day that I went back to work for Mrs. Weiss, and her house was still devoid of the piano playing; I watched her face a good deal, trying to read in her expressions what could have gone wrong with her musician. I tried to see in her eyes what the matter might be. I wanted beyond measure to ask her. I tried to determine if she seemed worried. I could not tell.

If I did not sense or know better, I might have thought that the musician was dead or dying; but was certain that I would have heard of or seen *that* on Mrs. Weiss's face. Of course if the musician had died, by way of the undertaker, the entire town would know it soon enough. Nevertheless, I had heard a little speculation since the piano had gone quiet, that perhaps the musician was dying. Because I believed that Mrs. Weiss's face would have given me hints to that story if it were true, I did not give any credence to it, though the idea did get me thinking about how much the music had come to mean to me. How could I live without it, now that I had heard it?

It had been well over a week before I heard the piano play again. I was overjoyed to hear it when the keys were finally touched once more. I had sorely missed that music. I welcomed its return with effulgent entirety. Life seemed quite lacking without that piano playing. Even while I knew that the musician did not play for me, I could still *feel* like the music was solely designed for my edification. At least I knew that I seemed to need that music as much as I needed food and drink, and rest.

I thought that I detected some tentativeness or maybe a weakness in the playing. I decided that the musician must have been sick at least that week and more. Yes, Mrs. Weiss's musician must have been taken ill, and perhaps with the fever that my children had just recovered from. As I thought about it, quite a few folks in the town and around had apparently been sick with the same complaint. Yes, the musician simply must have come down with the same illness.

As more days passed, it was as if I could hear the strength returning. The piano was played with more zeal, as I supposed that greater and then full health returned to the musician who played above where I sometimes worked. My worries over the musician dissipated into faded memories of the missing music, as the piano was played as before, and all seemed as it should be once more. Melodies drifted down from above.

9
Graveyard

When I felt the need for true solitude, I would sometimes go amongst the dead. There was a lady that I had liked very much; indeed, I would say that I had loved her as a very dear friend. Even though our friendship had been relatively short, I had felt close to her, and believed us true kindred spirits. She had some time ago died, and so I would visit her graveside, usually taking flowers when in season or some other token when I could. Sometimes I simply talked to her a little. And, I admit to talking to myself a little as well. I would also sometimes pray.

While there in the graveyard, oftentimes I would get lost in my own personal sorrows. The helpful thing of it was that I could cry or pray there, even somewhat aloud, for any passersby would only tend to think that I was lamenting the loss of my kindly friend. Yes, this friend of mine was now lost to me in this terrestrial realm, but the hopeful girl that I had once been was now seemingly lost to me as well. Who was I now? I barely knew. Where was she that I had been? Lost in the ethereal mist or more, it seemed to me.

When I would find myself lost in wondering things of 'what ifs', and I would regret a good deal the path of misery that my life had taken me on; if I did not think of my angel children, I might tend toward wishing to go back. I confess that I sometimes wished selfishly that I could go back and try again. I know it is not selfish to wish to leave a painful life, in a way, or I mean to say more to reclaim a happier time in a time gone by (or to try one's life once more); but, I say selfish because I cannot and should not wish to go back to take a different path that would not include my children. No, I will not regret my children for an instant. I would walk through fire for them and I would die for them, so why should I not also live this somewhat half-life of mine for them? Living for my children is the least that I can do for them. Their lives are my life. Without them, I would not wish to live.

I know that it is a sin to wish to die, or at least I think that it is; but in my lowest moments, I know that if not for my children, I would wish to leave this mortal probation rather than to stay married to that man. Would Heaven take me back? I do not know. I would hope I could belong there again somehow. I know that my children are worthy of Heaven, angels still as they are. Thus, perhaps if I am worthy of them as their mother, I can be worthy of the Heavenly place of which they still seem to belong to.

It is difficult not to become lost in my own pain and loneliness, but my little girl and boy always have their ways of calling me back to remember them as I should. When they are sad, hurt or sick, and even when they only need my attention in some other less urgent way, I am pulled out from my inner sorrows to focus on the needs of my daughter or son. I can be happy living in my children's lives instead of my own, in a way.

Here now, I am in this married lot, and so for my children, so be it. I suppose what I was trying to say is that I often wonder if I had chosen more carefully in marriage, could I be far happier now? And if I were happier, my children would be happier as well. If I had married better for myself, all would now be better for my children as well as for me. I should think that as a happier and fulfilled wife, I could be a far, far better mother. But I cannot lament for long. I cannot long think of what might have been, if only I had married better. And if I had married better, would I have been blessed with these same two children? I do think so, but I simply do not know.

I don't know why, but the graveyard seemed almost a place of worship to me, like a church, I suppose. As I have mentioned, the graveyard, which was somewhat on the edge or outside of town, was one of my places for solitary prayer, and even prayers that I could mutter aloud, fully attended by my heartfelt tears of sorrow.

You might think of this custom of mine quite strangely, my dear reader, but I did not tend to draw attention to myself when I spent time crying or even simply talking in the graveyard. Indeed, the few people who ever saw me there would intentionally leave me alone to my words with the dead or the apparent wailings over my loss as they supposed, thinking I lamented my friend who was now gone, or perhaps wondering if there was a family member that I was mourning. I was left to myself there in the town's cemetery. Other folks respected my solitude while I was there amongst the graves, even if I was not silent while appearing to pay my respects.

Do not mistake me. I did not make a frequent habit of blubbering or muttering in the graveyard. No, I only found myself there when I felt the clouds of darkness overshadowing my heart or mind. I only went to the graveyard in desperation to share my spiritual or other burdens with the dead because there was no living soul to whom I could speak to aloud about them. I had no friend to talk to. My mother-in-law was more in the way of a fairly kind acquaintance, my father-in-law was gone almost as much as my husband and I barely spoke to him at all; and since it was my husband who was the source of all my suffering and woes, of course I could not share my aching head or heart with him in any way at all.

When I sometimes became lost in my own despair, I would say or pray things that I might be ashamed of. One of these times, I was so low and lost in a river of my own tears, that I actually prayed thusly, "Oh, my Father, who art in Heaven, why hast thou forsaken me? Would that I had *died* at age seventeen. If I had left this mortal sphere, as my dear friend here has done, instead of *marrying* that man, I would have avoided a world of sorrow. I almost wish for death now. Oh, please, dear God, I beg thee, take me back to your sphere. Do not leave me *here* in this despairing misery."

And then I checked myself, with reality shaking me into reason, "Please *forgive* me, oh Lord, for my selfish moments. I do not regret my beautiful children. I could *never* regret my beloved little ones. They are my *only* true joys since thou hast blessed me with them. I thank thee for showing me a love I never knew before. I live for them. Please help me to live *better* for them. Please help me to think more of them. Please help me to think less of myself. Please help me to endure. Please help me to be worthy of my angel children. Please help me to be a good mother to them. And please, dear Lord, protect us. Please protect us from the cruelty and sins of my husband. Please especially protect and bless my children."

If the trade was necessary, I confess, I would choose to go through or to Hell that my children could return to Heaven. What did I care of myself, truly? I did not usually care about me and what my end might be. I suppose that this was some type of sin in itself. If to despair is to turn one's back on God, I suppose to give up on one's-self is a similar sort of sinning. It is surely not a good thing. But I did care greatly for my children, and so I knew that I should try to care for myself as well. I was their mother, after all, and how could a miserable woman make the best kind of mother? I knew that I must rise from the dead in a way, to live well: even my very best, for my children.

10
Mrs. Weiss

She had seemed cold or at least terribly reticent when I had first met her. Taciturn, I think would have been the word that I could have used to precisely describe Mrs. Weiss, before I truly came to know her more. Indeed, I had thought her even unkind in a way; but in a short time I had come to see her as only fiercely protective of the musician upstairs.

She was keeping the secret the best that she knew how, in a way that she obviously thought that she must. She was leaving the musician to his or her music. I came to believe that it was love: a motherly kind of love. Before I knew for certain, I fully believed that Mrs. Weiss was the musician's mother.

I imagined all the likely possibilities regarding the musician upstairs and I put myself in the place of Mrs. Weiss. 'What would I do, if the musician was my own child', I would ask myself, and I knew that the answer was very likely much like what Mrs. Weiss was doing. I would not care if I seemed eccentrically strange or even silly to the entire town, if what I did was to surround my child with whatever protection he or she needed for as long as was necessary.

Obviously the musician wanted to be left alone to play music. Whether the musician was injured, physically or emotionally, perfectly secluded cosseting was the desired medicine. A sheltered confinement was evidently the chosen remedy. And I thought that in time, the musician would finally come out of hiding to make peace with and join in the world again.

If however, the musician was an aberration or something in the way of abnormal or even akin to unnatural, such as a person with a hideous deformity (whether as born or later caused); perhaps the town around the piano house would never meet the musician after all. Maybe the piano player had never met the world in person, face to face, and intended to never do so. I could certainly put myself in the place of the musician's mother. I would do as she was doing. I would protect and love my child, no matter how old in age we both got to, and no matter how strange it all might seem to those beyond my own family walls.

One day as I steadily stitched for Mrs. Weiss whilst she intermittently talked, as I was listening to the piano playing from upstairs (trying all the while to seem to only be hearing my employer's voice), she simply stated, "You are not happy."

I was taken aback and looked up from my work suddenly, "What?"

"You are not happy working here?"

"No, no. *Yes*, of course I am. It is very pleasant work: very easy work. You pay me very well for my hours and efforts. I have as much time and more energy for my children than before I began working for you. I am *quite* happy working for you. Truly, I am."

She paused momentarily in thought, even as I thought about how I loved to stitch with the beautiful and even melancholy music playing in the house. Time stood still in a way, even as it sped by. I could mend or sew anything while the music played. And besides that fact, the intermittent conversation of Mrs. Weiss was generally pleasant enough as well.

She began again, "But, you are not happy about… *something*."

I wondered if I dare confess much, if anything at all, but decided it would do no harm to tentatively share a little of myself, "To be sure, I am not as happy as I could be, with *some* things."

"I do not wish to intrude upon your privacy of feelings, but, do you mind me asking, *what* things?"

I tried to begin again, "I love my children. They are my one true joy in life. My mother-in-law is good enough to me and wonderful to my children."

I wanted to say that the music upstairs was another joy.

She asked, "But your father-in-law?"

I answered, "No, I barely see or talk to him. He is hardly there."

"Your husband?"

I stumbled of breath before managing, "He is seldom home either."

"And *that* makes you unhappy? His absence is difficult for you?"

Without really thinking I bluntly stated, "Not at all."

She looked a little shocked, perhaps. She certainly had not expected that, I thought. Yes, at first she seemed quite astonished at my answer, and then a curious brow followed the surprised one. I did not know quite what to say and it seemed that Mrs. Weiss felt likewise, at least briefly.

Of course I knew that I could have said a good deal of how horrid my husband was, but I did not know if she would really want to hear all that type of miserable thing from me, and I knew that in good or higher society, it would not have been deemed very appropriate in such a conversation.

Mrs. Weiss cleared her throat, and then, "As you *know*... as you *well* know, there is a good deal of talk around the town about my household."

I shrugged more than nodded. I did not really like to admit it.

She continued, "Well, I don't know if you know that there is a little talk about *you* as well."

I shrugged and nodded at once, and in that instant my eyebrows rose as well.

She lowered her voice into a diminutive whisper, "They say that your husband is a bit of a brute, and *then* some."

Well, since the subject was out in the open at her own wishing, I decided to simply confess, "*Yes*, truth be told, I thank the Heavens above for *every* day that he stays away: every *hour*, in fact."

What a relief it was to breathe such words to a living soul! Even saying those few words was so very liberating to me. I was thankful to Mrs. Weiss for opening up the topic for me.

She said more, "Well, I did not like to believe any rumors, but now that you have echoed them a little, perhaps I will feel free to say a little more. I hear tell that the son takes after the father somewhat, and some people in the town tend to think that you are more like the mother."

My brow rose again, "Oh?"

"Yes, and that is a compliment to *you*, my dear Isabelle, because everyone thinks very highly of the elder Mrs. Ramstock, you see, and therefore of you as well. They simply do not think well of the two Mr. Ramstocks. Not at all, I assure you. The town pities you and your mother-in-law, but perhaps more especially *you*, I understand."

I had not previously known that anyone and especially many in the town knew even a hint of my troubles, but of course I was not surprised that some might know or at least suspect something. I had seen that my husband had at least generally learned his bad ways from his father, though I did think that my lot was worse than my mother-in-law's. I had never seen my father-in-law hit her. He was quick to be sharp, or angry or loud with her, or sometimes even to swear at her, but I had not seen him hit her like their son frequently did to me.

But then again, I suddenly realized that my husband never struck me in front of them either. My beatings were always a very private affair. That torture was saved for the bedchamber, and usually at night. What a new light this shone on my husband's mother. I suddenly cared for her all the more.

Mrs. Weiss had more to say, "Well, my dear. It is many a kind soul who is fooled into a sad marriage. Do not mistake me, though. I do not call you a fool, Isabelle. Not at all, I assure you. I only mean to say that good people can be caught by bad people in marriages. I fear that it happens *all* too often."

I only answered with, "I suppose so, yes."

She continued, "In point of fact, I tend to think that very selfish and unfeeling people tend to prey upon the kindhearted and tender souls such as yourself."

I could not think what to say but only managed, "Well…"

"I hate to say it like this, and so forgive me my forward bluntness, but I am an aging tired woman and speaking my mind when I can is one of my luxuries: thank the Heavens above that both the Mr. Ramstocks are gone off so very much so that you and the elder Mrs. Ramstock can enjoy some peace in the home."

I could not but nod and, "Well, yes." I certainly could not argue the point.

Mrs. Weiss smiled, "Sometimes the kindest thing a cruel person can do is to go away and stay away as much as may be. And forever is oftentimes the very best thing."

I only smiled in return.

Her face showed a loving concern, "And your children? Your beautiful children? I've noticed them at church, you see. They look angelic treasures to me. You are very blessed to have them. And you have made your mother-in-law a happy and proud grandmother. How do your beloved children do in the situation?"

"I think that they are fine. They hardly know anything is amiss. Their grandmother, my mother-in-law, is wonderful with them. She adores them. Yes, I am richly blessed in them. They are my reason for living."

She smiled the warmest smile I had ever seen upon her face, "Yes. The love of a mother for her children is unparalleled. Well, it should be. Sadly it is not always so. I cannot comprehend anything but loving one's children with one's very life."

I saw a generously sized tear in her eye nearest me, and my own tears were welling too. I could hardly choke out, "Yes. Very true."

As if on cue, we each turned from the other to wipe away the salty droplets from our eyes.

And the musician played my song once again.

11
Shenanigans

One day, I suddenly decided to ask the parson if I could make an exchange. My proposal was to be that I would clean the church weekly, so that I might have access to the piano there for my own practicing. I was happily surprised when he told me that I could come to play the piano whenever convenient for me if my timing was not in any interference with whatever else might be going on at the church building. In fact, he also invited my children to come play quietly if they could, while I practiced.

The parson's word of exchange to me was that if I practiced enough, perhaps someday he could call upon me as the substitute player for hymns on some Sundays. What a bargain that was. Though the thought of playing publicly at this point in my life struck fear into my soul, I could not but agree to such a deal. What a good man he was. His benevolence showed in his generously kind offer to me.

I think that I need not explain that the musician had inspired me to play piano once again. I did not wish to count the years since I had played. I feared that I could not remember a fraction of the songs that I used to play which had been committed to my memory so seemingly long ago. I doubted I could recall any of the songs that I had composed myself. Though, I could start. I could begin to play again. I certainly could try.

My children were delighted with the prospect of playing in the church while I played the piano there. Of course I explained to them the limitations or restrictions they would be held to. They could not be irreverent. I told them that they could not become loud nor could they run about wildly. Even though it was not on Sundays that we went, it was still a church. Nevertheless, I did not think it blasphemous if my little children danced near me with a little joy as I played some songs. I could not prevent them from swaying to the music. I did not like to tell them not to move their feet as well. The parson was as forgiving as could be, for he had a good portion of children of his own. He fully understood the lively innocent natures of young children.

One thing that my children loved to do, as became a quick habit when they came with me to the church for my piano practice, was to have their dolls and toys dance to my music. I thought this a welcome exchange for their possible wildly frolicking round and about instead. Yes, dancing dollies seemed somewhat better than frolicking children.

For the most part, little Lorna and tiny Alan played fairly quietly at my side as I played the piano. They chattered, but rarely any sounds above the noise of my halting stilted playing (my fumbling about on the keys). They played with any toys we had brought for them. They even nibbled on the bread, cheese or whatever I had brought; and they sipped water from the bottle I always carried.

Over a little time, my dear ones became very comfortable in the church. It became as if their very own. They had become accustomed to going there to that building quite often. Of course, they had long and always known the structure for Sundays, with all the other folks in town who attended the worship services on the Sabbath. But now, the church held another meaning to my children. It had been given something of a different special feeling to them. They seemed to think it their exclusive play place. Once or twice a week, they would toddle along with their mother to go to church when near nobody else would be there. They had the church all to themselves, as they felt.

I think that I enjoyed that kind of a feeling as well as my children did. To have the piano and the building to myself, with my children free to enjoy themselves, there was a particular joyfully relaxed feeling to me. Having no house of my own, making myself at home with my children at that church building, was our own little time and piece of paradise.

Of course, in their grandmother's house, when only she, they and I were there: we all felt a peaceful happiness amongst us. I could not complain about my mother-in-law and the general feeling of freedom in her house when she was entirely in charge of all of us. There was certainly abundant love in attendance. But I was still in my mother-in-law's house, my children were under their grandmother's roof, and I could not forget that it was not my own home. I was not at total liberty. I could not make the rules of the place: my children and I were living within the social structure or microcosm of a particular culture that was not exactly of my own making. I did not hold entire sway over my own or my children's destinies. I could not help but be reminded of this fact in little ways from time to time. I confess, dear reader, that I did occasionally crave a home of my very own.

I did feel a little of an unusual-to-me autonomy when my children went to the church with me on other than Sundays. I liked that independent feeling. I felt wholly like a mother. Because of this new or renewed sensation, I determined to take my children off and away with me more often: not to avoid their grandmother's influence, for her example was certainly a good enough one, but simply to remind my children and I that we were our own little family, as well as belonging to the larger family unit including their grandmother.

Sometimes I would become lost in my playing, and as I practiced on the keys of the church piano (remembering my songs of yesteryears), my children would become lost in their own playing. Indeed, they would almost become lost to me in the church. They would crawl and whisper, off here and there, between benches, behind walls and in corners. I would sometimes halt in my playing, in a little panic, wondering what mischief they might have gotten themselves into, or, far worse, fearing that they had left the building and run off and away somewhere.

Now and then, as mothers are prone to do, I would stop what I was doing to find and prepare to scold my children for any unwanted shenanigans. They were usually up to no harm, seldom up to no good, and often simply playing out of my ear and eyeshot.

One of their favorite games was to play preacher at the pulpit. At first I feared this playful pretending to be irreverently blasphemous, but when I asked the parson about it, he assured me that his own children had done just such a thing many a time as well. In fact, he happily thought that there might be a parson in the making amongst one of our sons someday.

And so, I allowed my children to take their turns at being little preachers. Their sermons were often delightfully entertaining to me. Indeed, I would tend to stop my playing at those moments simply to hear what they would have to say. And then, it might be me who would be scolded by the little preacher to keep playing the piano for their service. I was told by my children to play hymns for them as well. I did not mind that practice for I knew that the parson might cash in on my debt of playing for a Sunday service one day soon. Though I hoped that such a day would come later, if ever.

Oftentimes I could not decide which was more humorous: the sermons my children preached, or the hymns that they conjured whilst I played for them. They would sing of sun and clouds, of winds and birds, and of every manner of thing while I played any familiar hymn tune. They as much as told wild stories about the natural world around us while they sang aloud to the tunes from the Sunday hymnals. Little books in hand, they would pretend to read the words within as they chorused along.

These times alone with my children within the walls of the church were full of glorious moments to me. Do I dare confess, my dear reader, that I often felt more spiritually uplifted during some of those times with my children than I generally ever did during sermons in church? I would never say so to the parson, and it was certainly no personal slight to him and his preaching efforts or skills. I do not fear to say that my children were all the world to me, and having them to myself while they joyfully played was as much a Heavenly moment as anything could be.

The Sunday finally came when I was gently forced into publicly performing, or at least into rendering service at the black and white keys. I do not know why I felt so frightened before the fact. As a still young girl I had played piano for our children's Sunday school. Why was this so very different? I supposed my fears were mostly founded in my not having played in front of people, besides my children, in so very long; and I had mostly only ever played for children before. Well, there had been times when I had played piano and sang for adult company in growing up, but, now I was playing for a congregation at the parson's behest, and it felt so much bigger than anything that I had ever done before.

I overcame. I served, I endured. I would have certainly preferred to sit with my children in one of the back benches where I was usually more comfortable. Some folks in the church that day would have said that I played quite rightly. I had not done too badly, to be sure. The hymns had proceeded as they should. I had continued even when I had faltered a little. Perhaps few had noticed my slight stumbling. I had played so that all could sing. That day, my fingers had basically earned their reward of my former practicing. My songs came out all right for a modest player, but I surely did not shine. I was all nervousness.

I suppose that my only true consolation was that the musician was not in attendance to hear how badly I thought I had done. The musical child of Mrs. Weiss never attended Sunday services. At least, as yet, this person of mystery never had been part of the congregation in our little town church. Lucky thing for me too, for how miserable would my playing have been if the musician had been there to watch and hear my attempts at the piano. I would have been mortifyingly nervous, to be sure. Thank Heavens the musician had not yet come to our church.

12
From the Window

More than likely it was my imagination playing tricks upon my mind, but I thought I began to notice that certain especially wonderful songs (or at least the performances of them) were dependably cascading from that upper window whenever I went to and from the house. I also noticed beautiful or impressive songs playing continuously when I was *in* the house.

It almost seemed or felt as if the musician was playing for me, or playing *to* me. I suppose I liked to think of the pianist sometimes playing with me in mind. At least I thought that the piano player wanted to be heard. This grown child of Mrs. Weiss did not wish to be seen, but needed to be heard. Or, perhaps it was only my imagination. I did not know what was actually true, but I enjoyed the music nevertheless.

Once I had noticed that the best music seemed more consistently playing when I was coming to, within the walls of, or leaving the piano house, I could not help but pay all the more attention to what was being played. The songs that the musician consistently played seemed to have changed lately (since I had been coming to the piano house). I found myself wondering if the musician was specifically attempting to communicate something to me, even if only subconsciously. Did this person feel the same connection towards me as I felt towards him or her? Not likely, still I could not help but wonder.

Now, I had fully come to a point where I believed that the

musician was definitely a child of Mrs. Weiss. I had no proof, but something inside me seemed to tell me this was so, and so I believed it to be true. Then again, I infrequently supposed or speculated that the musician could have been one of her siblings, or a brother or sister of her husband. I could not imagine who else the musician might be, in relation to Mr. and Mrs. Weiss: a cousin, a ward, or some other person who was dependent upon them. Though, I always came back to feeling assured that the one who played piano upstairs, was indeed a child of my employer.

I still did not know whether this offspring of Mrs. Weiss was a son or daughter, I had never asked as yet, and she had never chosen to tell me. Indeed, she had never admitted to there being anyone upstairs playing the piano, the violin or any other instrument at all. I continued in the pretense of there being no noise whatsoever coming from above. We talked as if no one played.

It seemed supremely strange to me that Mrs. Weiss could ignore the music, or at least pretend so well that it was not emanating from that upper set of rooms. I could not really fathom how she could not show how much she must enjoy the wonder of it. There was a musical genius playing in her house, after all. And that musical genius was mostly likely her own child. Of these things I was increasingly assured.

I could not imagine sitting and pretending that a child of my own was not playing as if performing in a grand concert hall in Europe or out east in some great city, with a crowd of adoring listeners present. The music was certainly worthy of applause and great praise. The musician was worthy of an audience, and a very large one too, I thought.

Sometimes I wondered, maybe at some point in time in the recent or more distant past, if the musician had actually played in some concert hall somewhere, whether in the east of our country or in Europe somewhere. I could easily imagine that. Some time before whatever tragedy had struck, the musician must have played somewhere. This kind of music could not always have been played in such solitude. Could it have? How could that be possible? It seemed so very impossible to me.

The entire thing was a wonder to me. It was a curiously strange puzzle. I was in the midst of a true conundrum. Mrs. Weiss was obviously a part of it. Mr. Weiss, though rarely seen by at least me, must also surely be a part of this mystery of the musician. Why did the musician hide? Why the musician *played* did not seem much of a mystery to me. The pianist was a true master at it, and was compelled to play, *that* I was certain.

And it seemed a certain thing to me that once upon a time, far or further away, the musician had played for those with true trained ears to hear the mastery of the playing. The rich, the noble or the regal: these are those who must have once watched and listened as the musician played. I could easily picture Kings and Queens or the President of our country in attendance. Truly I could. Was I only imagining something great for a soul whom I believed held greatness? Perhaps, but this music was certainly loftier than from whence it came at present.

Sometimes I thought it a true tragedy that this wonderful musician played in such solitude and only those in or near the piano house were an audience to the concert-worthy music that flowed down the staircase, or out and down from that window. As for me nowadays, I mostly heard the brilliant music flowing down the inner stairs of the Tudor style house. Feeling a somewhat or almost an intimate part of the piano house, I oft happily worked there, where the musician played.

13
Mrs. Ramstock

They were my little angels on earth. They were everything to me. I often grieved for little Lorna and Alan and the lesser life that they knew. Yes, I believe that I loved them as much as any mother could, and they also had an adoring grandmother. I say adoring, and I suppose I could say indulging, for their grandmother Ramstock did spoil my children to a degree. I confess that I did not mind. I think I tended to feel that my children deserved a little spoiling to make up for their other losses. They barely had any kind of a father, I cannot say much about their grandfather, my parents and siblings were not in the picture of my nor my children's lives for various reasons, and I was not nearly as attentive to my children's every waking moments as I would have liked to have been.

Maybe if I had felt more secure or had more faith for my future, I would not have worked at all or at least as much as I did. But I feared and worried for my future and that of my children, and so I worked to save money for whatever 'rainy day' of needs that might come. I knew that I could not depend upon my husband for *anything*. I did not know if Grandmother Ramstock would or could always feed and shelter us. That is to say, I knew or at least was very certain that as long as the elder Mrs. Ramstock drew breath, she would care for her grandchildren and I could not imagine her throwing me out, but she would not live forever. Would she live long enough to be our guardian as long as we needed? Who could say what her husband would do, and I could imagine most anything untoward from my own horrid husband if his mother were not alive to intervene in some way.

Yes, my children's grandmother was a sort of friend to me. However, there was a certain distance between us. I suppose she was quite a good mother-in-law, as far as they go, from what I have heard. Yes, I think that I should say that she was a very good mother-in-law to me. She was almost as good as a mother might be. She was better than my own mother, I dare say. My mother Ramstock cared for me more, I could talk to her more, and she loved my children more. Nonetheless, in most respects, the reality was that she could never truly be more to me than a mother-in-law and my children's grandmother. She could only ever be a sort of friendly acquaintance, I could say.

It was the circumstance, you see. Had her son been an honorable man and my own beloved partner, I would not think as I do. Had he been a proper husband to me, I could have been and felt so very much closer to his mother. Even still, how close can you truly be to your husband's mother? You cannot complain about her son to her. You cannot tell her many things pertaining to your marriage that you might tell another woman of whom you felt perfectly secure with and personally close too. I had no confidante of this kind. I would have liked to have my mother or sisters to lean on, but I did not. It was not possible.

If I had any woman to fully and safely confide in, I would not complain about the elder Mrs. Ramstock. I would not deride my mother-in-law. That sort of thing would have been terribly ungrateful of me. No, I counted my blessings where she was concerned relative to me and especially my children. Yes, I was especially thankful that she adored my children.

Nevertheless, as a woman-to-woman thing, I could not confide on any deep level about any personal subject to my mother-in-law. I think I could say that I could not truly confide in her at all. I kept to myself in a definite way. Though I lived in her house and talked to her of many things, most particularly about anything relating to my children, I did not open up my heart to my mother Ramstock.

I could not. So much pressing on my heart in the way of pain and torment had everything to do with her son, you see. I could never truly talk to her about the most vital things pertaining to myself, because she could not see her son as I did. She saw what she wanted to see while I saw the unhappy reality. She saw the best things. I saw the worst.

Only once did I ever try to speak to the elder Mrs. Ramstock in a painfully honest way regarding her son, and to begin, I had said something akin to this, "What am I to do when he is so especially friendly with other ladies? I am mortified when he flirts with other women, and it is particularly painful when he does it in front of me. Could you speak to him for me? Maybe he would listen to *you*."

Her answer to me spoke volumes, I thought, "Well, you know, we wives must exercise *patience* with our husbands. They will come around eventually if we do. It is not our place to scold them. We must only *love* them."

I almost dared not, but boldly said anyway, "But you have been a loving and patient wife all these years and I do not see that your *own* Mr. Ramstock treats you as well as he should."

She looked embarrassed but recovered herself quickly, "He treats me well enough, I suppose, you know, as far as most husbands go. He pays for this house, and my food and clothing. That is certainly something to be grateful for. He is not perfect, but I can endure his imperfections. You must learn to *endure* as I do, and have done with it."

I felt inner anger and frustration but tempered my thoughts, "I don't *wish* to endure not being treated as though I am loved as a wife should be. Yes, there are worse husbands, but should not we expect, hope, pray and *insist* on better? Can we not demand better treatment?"

She shook her head and changed the subject to speak of something pleasant like the weather or a new dress or some such thing as that. I never broached the subject of unfit husbands or anything near to it again. I never complained of my husband to her since. I never asked for her help or her advice regarding my husband or marriage again. In point of fact, I do not think I ever spoke about her son to her since that day. At least, I tried not to, and I am certain that I never brought up anything relative to her son to her with regards to me.

Sometimes the elder Mrs. Ramstock might mention when she expected her own husband or her son to come home from this or that trip, or perhaps she would mention her or my husband for some other such innocuous reason, but we never talked of what was wrong with our marriages again. And I certainly never bothered to even hint towards there being anything wrong with her son and his treatment towards me. I did not think that she liked to admit to herself that there was anything amiss, either with her husband or especially their son.

Those were the parameters that I was forced to face about my relationship with my mother-in-law. Now, I could talk for hours to her about her grandchildren, for they were my children, and I had nothing but happy things to say. She preferred that I talk of little Lorna and Alan. With Grandmother Ramstock, I quickly came to prefer to only speak of my children to her as well. That was all generally happy talk. It was comfortable between us. There was no unpleasantness there. We could also talk of the weather or of clothing, décor or food, but never unpleasantness, particularly pertaining to the two men in her life. In the Ramstock house, the Ramstock men became as much as a non-subject.

And with those two men, the two Mr. Ramstocks, almost always gone off and away on business and who knows what else, it was better to not think or speak of them. They would each be home all too soon anyhow, and then the Ramstock household revolved entirely around either man, or any of their whims. They usually came home separately. It was better that way I came to understand.

Sometimes, such as at Christmastime, both Ramstock men would come home simultaneously. Christmastime and other times that those two men came home at once, was not the blissfully happy holiday it was meant to be, for they would invariably argue.

They would tend to get loud in their arguments. The children would always be frightened at the shouting that happened in the house, and I tried to shield their ears from the swearing as well.

It always amazed me the way the elder Mrs. Ramstock would attempt to soothe both savage beasts at the same time. She would, 'Now, now' and 'There, there' while I would leave the room, leaving those Ramstocks to their own particularly unpleasant ways. I would have *none* of that; and I would not subject my children to it. I would take my children to their room and explain it all away with 'the drink'. What else could I say? I did not know what else to say. I would soothe and comfort my children the best I could in any way that came to me in those moments in time. I would have liked to drive them far away forever, but that was not possible in the least. I had no one and nowhere else to take my children to.

The Ramstock house was two different places. When Grandmother Ramstock was entirely at the helm, it was certainly all pleasantness. When either of the Ramstock men were home and in charge, as they always were inclined to be when home, it was just the opposite. When both men were home at the same time, it was constant friction and contention. Those were the days that, if I possibly could manage such an outing, I took my children out on long walks or to the church to play within, as I played the piano.

Beyond the one attempt to begin to share with my mother-in-law, the depths of the cruelty of my husband and how I felt he continually disgraced me, it was as if there was a dividing line between my mother Ramstock and me. I left her to her son as she liked to think of him. I knew what he truly was relative to his treatment against me. He was not a husband. He was a cruel owner. But I supposed that my mother-in-law was blinded to the harsh and cruel ways of some men, by her own coping with her own ill-behaved husband.

For all that my mother-in-law was *not* to me, she was a wonderful grandmother to my children. Indeed, she was completely joyful in their care. I could always depend upon her to tend to my children while I worked for a part of my living, and savings towards whatever the future might hold for me and my children, without any regard to my husband. I did not like to call him my own, but what else was I to do? He was my husband and that was my own sad reality.

The elder Mrs. Ramstock could not possibly be my true friend in the way of knowing my sorrows and sharing my burdens. Her son would always be foremost in her loyalties if it ever came to the point. She would never take my side over or against him, and I fully knew it. In that way, I was always on my own. I was alone in the world. Except for my children, of whom I was prime protector, I was living a lonely life, a life alone, in the Ramstock house alongside my mother-in-law.

14
A Husband

Somewhat like his father, my husband was usually gone off on supposed business. He was not my own. I was his, as owned, to be sure, but I did not truly have a husband as I considered such to be, at least as ordained by God and as expected by humane and civilized beings. The law in our day and age might be a different thing in differing territories and countries. A man could get away with certain treatment where his wife was concerned. I supposed that some wives might find ways to manipulate to their own selfish and ungodly ends as well. I was not made of such things. I was an honest being who wished to tell the truth as I saw it. I wanted to deal plainly. I simply wanted a simple happiness with an honest husband.

Whether or not the elder Mr. Ramstock did more than mere business dealings in his travels away, there was plenty of evidence from what I knew to prove that my own Mr. Ramstock often chose to go off gambling at least and likely carousing as well. Such indulgences, or even things I would call debauchery, were committed by my husband regularly, I thought. I know not of my husband's every action for certain these days, but I can surely guess, and be assured that I surmise close to the mark.

Did my husband conduct any true business on any of his business trips away from home? I thought not. There was no money to show for his time away. At least I never saw any income. If he did make any coin in any business effort, perhaps it was thrown away on gambling or spent on other women.

No, he never did truly admit to anything. But, yes, there had been evidence enough along the way. And the look on his face whenever I accused him of certain wayward things, told the truth of it all to me more and better than his words could have ever clarified. He did not fully deny many a sordid thing that I told him I was assured that he had been up to while away from me. His usual reactions were to either laugh at me for feeling mortified at his life actions and my own life connection to him, or to hit me and hard for figuring him out.

I was young and naïve when I was easily convinced by my parents to marry the young Mr. Ramstock. It seems so very long ago but it is only perhaps a half dozen years I think: little more, anyway. I do not count the anniversaries. I do not wish to remember how long it has been that I have been chained to that ungodly man. I only thank God and Heaven above that my illicit husband chooses to be gone from me so very much. Saints be praised for that miracle of miracles in my life.

My husband was once all things handsome and charming. I thought that he loved me and I knew that if he did, I could love him. My heart would have been bonded to his own firmly, if only he had treated me rightly. But he was far too self-serving to be true to our vows of marriage and togetherness. He was far too short and hot tempered to treat me gently.

The sanctity of our marriage was fairly promptly corrupted to fit his whims. My mind and heart were of no concern to him. I often wondered why he had ever married me at all. I did not think him ready to wed. Perhaps he never would have been. There are surely men like that: men who should never dare to marry. To inflict themselves on most any decent woman is a tragedy beyond simple sin. As to any woman who is like unto and deserves such a man as my husband, I do not comprehend that sort of female.

Why did my husband choose to go to the trouble to marry me? A habitual tradition he thought he might try out for a time? He thought he should finally get himself a wife? But he was still young. He saw a little of his mother in me perhaps? Yes, quite likely. A

woman easily molded to fit into whatever shape he wished? Did he
want children? I did not think as much now: not since what I had
seen in these years as his wife and the mother of his two children. I
could not piece together the puzzle as to why he married me in the
first place. Perhaps he thought it an amusement. Maybe I will never
really know. My husband does not ever really talk to me. Beyond
the darkness that I have seen hiding, he has never shown me what
all is in his mind or heart.

I had lost track as to how long it had been since my husband
had been home. I had breathed easily for quite some time now. I
had gotten so pleasantly used to his lengthy absence this time. In
fact, he had been gone so long that his father had come and gone
at least twice since we had seen the son. Though now, without any
warning, he had finally returned. My husband was come back.

As had recently become my usual practice, I instantly moved
myself into my children's room. This is what I now did whenever
my husband returned home. I left our bedchamber to him; and
to him alone. I knew that this fact angered him to no end, but
I clandestinely rebelled against him in this one particular way.
Yes, it was in large measure a total rebellion from a wife against
her husband. I would not submit. I would not be owned in that
bodily way. I was quite assured that he was not acting married to
me when he was away, and so I refused to play the part of wife at
night whenever he returned. That intimate part of our marriage had
passed into history a long while since.

I did not think that my husband truly or fully wished to be
with me in the nights, but he did not want his parents to know
this. For his sake I suppose, I tried not to make my move obvious.
I tried to keep it a secret between the two of us. I did not openly
revile and rebel against him. My children were still young enough
not to truly notice. They were asleep each night before I crawled in
beside them onto that big bed of theirs anyway. And they did not
think anything amiss if they awoke to find me there in the morning
or before, because I often lay down beside them to sing lullabies or
to talk softly to them before and as they fell off to sleep. They were

quite used to my presence in their room and were only too happy to welcome their mama in bed also.

Regardless of my husband's feelings, or more likely his pride, I did not care if his mother knew what I was doing. She looked the other way while her son treated me ill and so I left her to look the other way while I refused to sleep in the same room with her son. What the elder Mrs. Ramstock did with her husband was her affair, and mine was my own as well. I supposed that this was what we had all come to. We each lived our own sort or semblance of marriage. Mine was surely a sham or worse. And I certainly did not think of my husband's parents as an ideal married couple.

That first night after I had retired for my slumbers, my husband quietly knocked on my door, or as it was, our children's door, and somewhat whispering, and almost pleading, he said, "Are you coming to bed, Isabelle?"

Without opening the door, and with what had become my usual lie as a part of playing this game of pretending to still be living as if a wife to this man, I returned, "I will be there in a few minutes. Go to bed without me."

Perhaps five or ten minutes later, my husband surprised me by persisting with another knock at the door and more whispers, "Isabelle? Why aren't you coming to bed? What are you doing? I'm waiting for you."

I wondered at his second attempt. He knew the new habit I had begun between us. Why did he think this particular return home would be any different than it had been the last number of times? Did he suddenly love me in some way? Did he now wish to have me as his wife, to love, to hold, to keep? I thought not.

I played our game, "I just need to finish up a few things. Go to bed."

All was quiet outside the door for a few more minutes and then he was there again, almost begging, "Isabelle, I want to talk to you."

Exasperated, I decided to go to the door, which I opened a crack and then spoke only, "What?"

"What are you doing in there? Why aren't you coming to bed?

I've been waiting."

I shook my head and let down the pretense I had built between us, "I'm not coming to your room. I'm sleeping here."

He swore under his breath and then stated very bluntly, "You are my wife. I command you to come to our room, to bed."

I defied him, "You don't play the husband when you are away, and so I will not play the wife when you are home."

He slapped my face. My left cheek stung horribly. Tears welled up in at least that eye. My heart ached more than my face was hurting. This was not the arrangement I vowed to, but it was what I had long felt forced to come to because of him and all that he had done against me. What else could I do?

His voice rose a little beyond his prior whispers, "Come to our room, *now.*"

I risked being hit more and worse, "No."

I quickly ducked out of the way when he tried to slap me once more, and then I slammed the door shut in his face. I locked him out. He began banging on the door. He was yelling now. Between his noise-making, I heard his mother in the hallway asking what the matter was. The children were rousing. Then I heard my mother Ramstock pleading with him to simply go to bed. I supposed that she might have thought that we had simply quarreled, if she did not know the entire truth of what I had decided a while back. The war was over for tonight, though I still felt the fear in my heart and the heat on my face where his hand had struck. Could I sleep tonight? Not likely for a while at least. I would weep and worry at length yet.

15
Corruptions

The following day was a chilly one. The weather outside was perfectly fine, but the tensions between my husband and I were very thick inside the house. My poor mother Ramstock tried to flit and flutter around with happy talk and gracious smiles. She always liked to smooth the way for peacefulness. I soon decided to leave the children to their grandmother's care while I had it out to some degree with my husband. I openly suggested that little Lorna and Alan would enjoy playing outside in the yard under the watchful eye of their dear grandmother, and my always amiable mother-in-law quickly complied.

Because of past history with my husband, I believed that he would start something up as soon as his mother was out of earshot and I was right. He tore into me right away, "What is the meaning of last night? I come home tired and weary from a lengthy trip of business and you *refuse* to come to our room all the night through? Why are you refusing to behave as a wife *should*?"

I took a deep breath before beginning, "And do you behave as a *husband* should? It is the *nature* of your trips that have caused my change of habits regarding you."

He was instant defensive anger and his voice got loud at once, "The *nature* of my trips? The nature of my trips you say? What are you hinting at?"

"Only that we both know that you are up to no good when you travel."

His voice was louder and all the angrier, "No good? Up to no good?"

I calmly and very simply said, "Yes."

"I go away on *business*. You call that no good?"

"Perhaps you do a *little* business."

"Perhaps I do a *little* business? What else do you think I am doing?"

I felt a little bolder than usual, and so were my instantaneous accusations, "Drinking, gambling and dallying with women, or *worse*, I should say."

He was almost speechless. I readied myself to be hit. I expected to be hit, and to be hit quite hard. I did not care. Not at that moment. I determined within myself that I would wear the bruises with honor instead of hiding them in my own shame as was my usual practice.

He found his voice, and it was as loud as ever, "Dallying with women or worse? How *dare* you!"

"No, how dare *you*."

He seethed and swore, "I should knock your head off of your shoulders for that accusation."

"Do you deny it?"

"Of course I deny it."

"You do bad enough in front of my face and have since we were married. I wager you do far *more* out of my eyesight."

"*Bad* enough? What are you talking about?"

"All your flirtations with other women. You have always done it, and you *know* it."

He swore again and then said more, "I am *sick* of this subject. You have accused me of such before and I have always denied your claims."

"You can deny all you want, but I know what I have seen and I am certain of what I suspect."

"Oh, *what*? Harmless flirtations? Stupid wife. Men are wont to flirt with women. You should have known *that* fact long before I married you. What an insipid little innocent you were. And what a pious annoying prude you are now."

"Yes, I was innocent and naïve to think that you would be a faithful husband to me. I did not know you then, but I know you too well now."

He laughed, and then tried to taunt me in his way, "You know *nothing* of me. You only imagine what you think I am doing while I am away from you, but you will *never* know all that I do."

"Well, I know enough to live my own life regardless of you and what you do."

"Your *own* life? You think you can live your own life? *I own you,* and your *life.*"

"Yes, you own me. I am your wife. But, I can say *no* to some things. I am not your slave nor your mule."

He grabbed me roughly, "You can *say* no, but you have no power where I *insist.*"

I pushed him away forcefully, "This is your *mother's* house. This is no brothel. Have you no shame at *all*? Have you no *decency*? I know you care at least a *little* of what she thinks of you. Do not dare me to tell her *all* about you."

He looked outside to where his mother and the children were enjoying each other and the day, off and away enough not to hear much of what was going on inside the Ramstock house. My mother-in-law was prodigiously good at ignoring anything unpleasant relative to her son, and she had learned to distract her grandchildren. I was at least grateful for that on behalf of my children.

As usual in our arguments of this kind, my husband had admitted to nothing actual. He never admitted to anything of any truly serious nature. He never admitted to details. He did not seem to care if I *knew* anything. He only did not admit to anything. Indeed, he seemed to derive a strangely unnatural pleasure in knowing that he had injured me. His frequent goal seemed to be a want to pierce my heart. His greatest frustration almost seemed when he thought that he could not harm me in those ways. If he could not hurt me, he was not happy. I could not fully comprehend his sins or reasons for falling into them, but I was too tired to entirely try. I breathed deeply and looked away from him.

He chose to continue thusly, "And you think that I drink and gamble too much?"

I waxed painfully honest, "I would allow you to drink, but for the lascivious sins that tend to follow drunkenness. I would forgive any gambling but for the money that is almost always lost to no useful purpose. And these two things are nothing at all to breaking your marital vows to me with regards to other women. *That* is something too much for me to bear. I can even suffer your losses of temper and blows against my body, but I *cannot* live with your infidelities."

He first cruelly smiled, obviously feeling some wicked triumph, and then his brow furrowed in angry controlling, "You will live with whatever I choose to do. I will come and go as I please. I will do what and with whom I *want*."

"I *know* you will. I know that you do and have done. What of it? What is it to me *now*?"

"What do you mean by '*now*?'"

"I mean that I am not your subservient little controllable wife any longer."

"Oh, you *aren't*, are you? Ah, I think I see what is going on. You think that since you have made yourself the lowly beggarly washer woman in the town, you have a little coin and you will run away from me?"

"No, I only will not be tortured as I once allowed you to do against me."

His look was fully contemptuous detesting, "*Allowed* me? You think that *you* allow me? You are a little *nothing*. I can do with you as I want."

"In your mother's house there are limits to your powers over me."

"Yes, well, perhaps I will move us away to our own place again."

"And then, the moment you go off carousing, I will be gone to somewhere that you cannot find me."

"Will you indeed?"

"Do not force me to do it."

He breathed at length. I could see that he was thinking things through. I wondered what was to come next. He stared out the window. Once upon a time in our marriage he could use his sweet words with me. He many times garnered my forgiveness. We had come too far by now, though. He had turned my love for him into hatred and then eventually a deadness of feeling. He could not stir my soul like he once had the power to do. He could not work on me. He did not quite know what to do with me now, I thought.

He began again, "And, speaking of money, I do not like you working round about. You make me ashamed of you. You are making my family look bad. You do not need the money: you have everything you need here."

I defended my right to work, "I need a little coin of my own. You do not give me any money and I do not wish to burden your mother, asking for this or that little thing. Would *that* not make you feel ashamed?"

"Are you trying to insult me?"

"I am only stating facts."

"You work at my pleasure. I can force you to stop at any moment. You are my wife, and it reflects badly on me when my wife acts like a beggar."

I purposely minimized it in a kind of self-defense, "I work very little: I am mostly only doing a little stitchery now and then. Needlework is the pastime of ladies, after all. I need not work as a laundress any longer. I only need a few coins here and there. As I said, I don't wish to trouble your mother with my little needs now and then."

"Ladies do not sew for money."

"Well, I like to sew, and I am doing a good turn for another lady when I sew for her, and she does a good turn for me when she pays me a little coin. It is only a fair trade between friends so to speak."

He mulled it all over in his mind, and then, "And how much coin have you saved up?"

I outright lied, "I have made very little money. How could I possibly have saved up anything? A woman needs her little things and I sometimes like to buy sweets for the children. I do not turn to your mother for her spare change. I depend upon myself for such things."

I did not think he believed me. I feared that he would push the issue. He had found and taken my money before. I had learned how to better hide it. I knew it was not outside the realm of possibilities for him to try to beat the truth out of me. Still, I was determined. I would not yield. I would not give up my savings.

I thought to interject, "Think of it this way: your mother enjoys keeping her grandchildren to herself when I go out, and I'm sure she appreciates that I am not asking her for money."

"Well, I suppose there is some truth there. I will give you that. But you still dress like a pauper and I am ashamed of your appearance. Can't you try to dress a little better? But, then again, I suppose I ask too much of such as you. You have never had any good sense or taste, and no amount of money would give it to you anyhow."

I let him have his victory speech against my taste and sense. I did not bother to argue with him.

He thought to speak on another subject, "And what's this I hear of you taking my children to the church at all hours of every day and night? What are you up to there?"

I was relieved to be able to answer such an easy question, "I am only practicing my piano. And the children play near me there as I do. That is all. They enjoy it."

"They *enjoy* it, you claim? I would think that they would rather play at home with their grandmother watching out for them than to be forced to trudge all the way over to the church to be bored to death and ignored by you while you bang on the piano keys."

I chose a softer answer to his wrathful questioning, "Well, I do not have to take them with me. I would surely leave them with your mother if they wanted, and if she wished, but they always seem to want to come to the church when I go, and I thought that your mother might like a little rest from their noise and energetic play. We can certainly leave it to the children and your mother to decide. It is up to them if you like. I will never push them to come to the church with me when I go there to practice the piano. If your mother wants them with her instead, I will surely leave them with her."

He seemed appeased, at least momentarily. I wondered what might be next. I never knew for certain with him.

He suddenly announced, "Just don't give my children too much of that *church* and its goings on. I don't want them to turn out like *you*."

I tried, "They go to church with your mother more than with me. Sometimes I don't even *go* on Sundays. You *know* that your mother never likes to miss a week, and she likes her grandchildren to be there next to her."

"Don't be ridiculous. I know you are as regular a churchgoer as my mother, and you are far more pious too."

"But your mother…"

"Leave my mother out of this."

I was a little stunned. I did not know what to make of what he was saying. I did not know what he was trying to say to me. I feared that there was more to come from him.

He sneered strangely at me, "You just go ahead and take your little ones to church with you when you do. You give up *all* your possible moments of happiness for your children while they are young, and while *you* are still relatively young. You go ahead and waste your life while *I* live. I will pursue my own happiness and you may hold to your drudgery."

I felt that he was trying to sting me. He wanted me to feel ill-used I supposed. Perhaps he thought I could feel jealous of the life he was living as compared to mine. He was indulging his desires but I was denied all of those guilty pleasures in his view. He was gorging out in the world while I was left empty at home. I think he thought himself free while I was in bondage. Oh, how little he knew of what was really true and joyous in life.

I chose only to answer in this way, "I *will* hold to my children. *They* are my happiness. *Your* life's choices will not bring you true joy."

There was a chillingly cold look in his eyes as he continued, "Happiness, joy: these are just words. But, mark my words well, my wife; no matter what you sacrifice, I will have them later. I will undo all the supposed religious good you are trying to do now. I promise you that I will step in and corrupt them later on. I will do it to spite you. I will laugh as I do it. And there will be nothing that you can do to stop me from turning your precious children away from you and away from your God."

I felt a horridness standing in front of him, "Your mother will stop you if I cannot."

"Oh, she *will*, will she? And did she stop *me* from following in my father's footsteps?"

"You say that with such disdain. Who do you despise *more*, your mother or your father?"

"*Both*: he for his abuses and she for not protecting me from him."

I lamented to my husband, "I do not understand you."

"You never have and you never will, and I do not understand you. And there you are. We are at our usual mutual impasse."

"Why would you not protect your own children from yourself then; if you are anything like whatever it is that you dislike about either of your parents?"

I thought I saw a wetness welling in at least one of his eyes. Maybe it was only a kind of hope left in my heart.

He turned away just a moment and then turned back to say, "Oh, to the devil with you. What a *wife* you have turned out to be. You bore me to no end."

And my husband was soon gone away again. Of course, I gave thanks and hoped for a lengthy respite from more misery.

16
In the Window

J ust briefly, I saw him. He was watching me as I left. When I
looked up to the window, as I always did coming and going
from his piano house, I saw him standing there observing me.
In that instant, he stepped away from view. Yes, he was a man.
A young man I thought. Or had I only imagined him? I almost
thought that I had conjured him up. I barely saw enough of him to
know for certain what or who I had seen.

But, I *had* seen him. The musician was most definitely a man. I
was quite certain of that fact. Even still, then I began to doubt what
my eyes had told me in that fraction of a moment. Well, at least
I could be sure that the musician *looked* very much like a young
man. The only other possibility was that the musician was a young
woman dressed in the garb of a man. But why would a woman
dress to look like a man? Could the musician be a woman after all?
Would there be any sensible or justifiable reason for a woman to
try to appear to be a man? I could not help myself from wondering
these and all manner of questions surrounding the now old mystery
that had taken another turn, or at least revealed a little something
to me. Or so it seemed.

The next day that I worked for Mrs. Weiss at the piano house,
I watched for the young man, or possibly the young woman posing
as a man. Still, I was far more certain that the musician was male
rather than female. The former was far more likely than the latter.
Yes, I was very sure that he was not a woman. I did not see him
upon arriving, but I did see him watching me once again as I was

leaving. Only for an instant, really: as soon as I looked up to see him, he backed away, trying not to be seen. I was now all the more certain that the musician was a man.

The next time I came, I saw him in the window, as if he had been watching for me. Yes, I was certain that he was indeed a man and was looking out for my arrival again. I had seen him in the window from afar. He was watching the direction from whence I always came. Before I closed the distance between us, in order to watch him longer than a mere moment, I did not exactly look up at him. I kept my head somewhat down and looked up at him with only my eyes. I tried to appear uninterested in his general direction. I even tried to appear to be looking elsewhere. I forced my head to hint other than where my eyes were somewhat staring. In this, I was able to watch him a good while.

When I came close enough to the piano house that he might have been able to see, or perhaps *feel* my eyes gazing upon him, he backed away out of the window again. This incident caused me to wonder how many times the musician had watched me coming and going from his house. Had he watched me many a time before? Why was he watching me? Did he watch everyone passing by, or coming and going? Why would he watch *me* over anyone else?

I felt a strange sensation knowing, or at least believing that the musician had been watching me. It was not a bad feeling. I could not say that it was a good or thrilling kind of feeling either. One thing I can say is that I tried not to feel anything relative to him, *now*. Now that I knew that the musician was a man, and apparently a younger man, possibly near my own age, I told myself that I should take care not to have much in the way of any feelings regarding him.

I did not know if the musician was or had ever been married, I actually fancied not at all; but, *I* was. I was not happily married, to be sure; but, I *was* married. I was taken. I was owned. And though I did not live as if married, I could not live otherwise. I was not free. I could not allow myself to feel very much relative to the musician any longer. I knew that I should not think about the musician too very much any longer. I was quite unexpectedly saddened to realize that the musician was a man. If he had been a young woman, we could have someday become intimate friends. Or, at least I thought as much at the time.

I knew that I must change myself in future. I knew that I must now erect a wall around myself to guard against my former caring thoughts about the musician. I dared not care so deeply about his music as I had before. I could not care so much about the piano player. I knew that I needs must distance my heart from the musician; for I was unfortunately married, and the musician seemed certainly to be a fairly young man.

17
My Sisters

Dolores was a born flirt from the start, or at least as far back as I can recall. It seemed that she had always flirted with all boys first and then every man in the vicinity, young or older. I never knew why she was so very inclined towards such coquetry, but it was common knowledge that she was. Looking back, I think I could safely say that she got that improper tendency from our mother, certainly to some degree. I sometimes tried to encourage Dolores to temper her temptation towards such aimless and wide-ranging flirtations, but she would not be guided by me, even though I was her older sister. My parents absolutely would not check her, and so she was the coquette that she chose to be.

The overt friendliness of my sister was something that I had long gotten used to by the time my husband came along, and so when Dolores was what I might call dangerously friendly to my husband, I did not think much of it at first. It did not bother me, at first. Perhaps I forgave my sister more than my husband in those early days of their flirtations one with another, because I was used to my sister's old habits that I thought generally innocuous, and *she* had not solemnly bound herself in matrimonial promises to me as my husband so recently had. Still, should a sister not instinctively respect the sanctity of her own sister's marriage?

In those early beginnings of discomfort for me because of the two of them together, I first attempted to talk to my husband about his own behavior. He chose to blame it all on my flirtatious sister even as he at once claimed the total harmlessness in all of it. She was his new sister, after all. What possible harm could there be in his friendliness to her as her new brother? I warned of harm to our marriage. He could not be reasoned with on that point, in my own view.

Dolores was the foundation for that first very early quarrelling that occurred between my husband and myself. Though she did not know it (or at least I did not think that she knew or even imagined), my husband and I fought a good deal about her and what she enjoyed doing and saying with him. Their constant intimate cavorting was injurious, distressing and embarrassing to me.

The entire situation of the bad behavior of my younger sister began to show me what little fidelity my husband was made of right from the beginning. I could not get my husband to change his behavior towards my flirtatious sister (even with all my scolding towards him). In a kind of desperation, I attempted to speak with Dolores about it all, in the hopes that her station in life as my sister would propel her to at least try to corral her unguarded silliness towards my husband, for my sake. For me, could she not stop her flirtatious habits toward just the one man: my man? One would think that one's own sister would agree to some degree of propriety and mutual respect with regards to one's husband. Nonetheless, it was not so.

What I thought would have been the beginning to the ending of all of it, was the actual worsening of the problem. I was sadly mistaken in my plan, for forcing my sister to face the damaging consequences (of her dalliances with my husband), upon me and my heart, only made her proclivity to endear herself to him all the more and for the worse. Knowing that my husband had a wandering eye for certain, seemed to puff up her pride that he was focused on her *instead* of his own new bride, and her older sister. For her part, she reveled in the new information that I had so honestly and painfully confided in her. She thought herself higher than me because of all this. Knowing that my husband would not stop his cavorting with her became her ridiculous type of triumph over me. I had not thought prior that she could ever be so wrong in her heart nor so terribly cruel. But so she was.

Dolores proffered one key excuse to me that she thought fully excused herself, and that was that if my husband wasn't being overly friendly with her, he would be enjoying flirtatiousness with some other woman anyhow. Yes, this was in its part quite true, but that did not wash away her own little sin in the matter. I tried more than a few times in vain to remind her of the solemn sin of tampering with the sanctity of my marriage, but she proved herself proud to catch my husband's eye or glean any notice from him. This seemed to make her feel important or exalted somehow. What their behavior together did to harm me seemed to be of no account to Dolores.

After a short while I entirely accepted the sad reality that even if I was able to convince my sister to behave herself relative to my husband, I could not speak to every woman on earth. Halting the flirting between my sister and my husband would only be as if stopping one star from falling, so to speak. There was an endless sky of stars, was there not? Any woman willing to exchange flirtations with my husband would be part of my problems and pain, and I knew that I could not run around convincing every woman to behave herself where my husband was concerned. The solution lay at my husband's feet, and he did not wish to solve the problem he imposed upon me.

Even still, to have one's own sister flirting with one's husband is all the more excruciating than when he might flirt with any stranger along the way. The nearer contravention pierced deeper into the heart. I supposed that if a closest friend dallied with one's husband, the effect would be similar. Was it not bad enough for me and my poor heart that my husband would not control his friendliness with any woman that crossed his path? Yes, my heart was soon trodden upon continually. And thus was the beginning of the most vexing transgression I would suffer under, due to my husband's varied vices.

My other and older sister, the more reserved one, would prove unworthy as my immediate female kin in her own right. Irene was one who liked to be thought well of. While Dolores did not seem to care what people thought and said about her, Irene was just the opposite. She wanted to be held in high regard at all times. At first glance, one would think Irene my better sister and Dolores the naughty one; but things and people are not always what they seem at first. Appearances can often deceive.

You might think it horrid of me to say the following of my older sister, but full truth be told, Irene was a false being. Her visage was a sweet and innocent façade. I knew some of the real young woman behind that lovely mask, but I did not imagine the worst that lie beneath. As her sister, I knew her so very well, but I did not know her as one might expect. She had her secrets that I had no idea of.

In retrospect, I can now see Irene as obviously the more clandestine creature. She was more subtle in her game, I now suppose. Shockingly, it was *she* who I caught in a compromising position with my husband. Yes, to my great heartbreak and surprise, it was my seemingly innocent sister Irene who actually cavorted with my husband behind the curtains. If I could do it over again, would I attack them both in some way? I do not know; for at the time, I left them and their situation just as swiftly as I had discovered them. I ran off and away to cry alone and unseen, to hide from them the horrible pain that they had made me to feel so very deeply.

It should come as no surprise to you that I am in no way close to either of my sisters at present. Indeed, it was partially because of them that I so promptly and hopefully agreed to come west to live and then eventually to move in with my parents-in-law. When I first agreed to that lengthy and arduous journey, I had thought that the change in society and family associations, and getting away from my imprudent sisters, would free me from a less than perfectly faithful husband. It seemed a fresh start. I had hoped that a new life of better behavior on his part might begin. I had prayed that, removed from the temptations of my sisters, my husband would repent and become the husband that he should be to me. I had trusted that his parents would point him rightly. I was wrong.

My only later given and current consolation beyond my wonderful children and my kind mother-in-law is the fact that my husband's flirtations and whatever worse behavior he engages in are generally beyond my view. I am not overtly humiliated and publicly pained as I was before, when he toyed with my sisters and to all their mutual devilish delights. At least my husband takes his horrid habits to other towns. I can at least almost pretend publicly that he is not what he in actuality is.

Letters have been sent to my sisters by me from time to time, with them writing back very little. At least they wrote to say that they have both married since I left them. From what I have learned, I surmise that Irene trapped herself a good fellow with her masked manipulations. I feel sorry for him, but I hope that he can be happy with such a woman as her. I think that Dolores did not do so well, though she sang her husband's praises as being an uncommonly handsome catch.

Of course I wish both my sisters happy now and well in their future lives, but I do not hold out hopes that they will find genuine joy because of who they truly are. From what I have seen in my life's journey so far, it seems to me that few people ever really change. Yes, I believe in repentance, but I think it a hard road to walk that few people rise up to.

I would wish my sisters to repent of their ills and to finally find lasting happiness, but I leave that to them. No, they are not entirely or truly evil, or the worst kinds of devilish people, but they are surely not what I would call especially angelic. By what I have now just shared with you, dear reader, I might seem the heartlessly cold sister, but my attempts at being close to my sisters have been mostly, if not completely, to no avail. I have tried to reach out to them, but they obviously do not wish to reach back my way.

Forgiving both Irene and Dolores their improprieties with my husband came easily once I was gone from my sisters, but there has been little effort on their part to be friends to me since. I am alone in the world where they are concerned. I have learned over time that there is little point in my trying to find warmth with my sisters. Their hearts wax cold, I have found.

18
Saloons

Early on in my marriage, my husband often took me to saloons with him for evenings out. Even though I was not personally at ease in the atmosphere of a public drinking and dancing house; at first my thinking was that it was better for me to go with him there, than to let him go alone and without me. If he was determined to find his night's entertainment at a saloon, was it not best for me to accompany him, rather than to decline going? For then he might likely fill his belly with strong drinks; with dancing girls and worse females all around him. I dared not let the demon liquor rule my husband in such an environment without me there with him, to try to guide and guard him. I thought it my duty to help protect the sanctity of our marriage.

Besides, if I were to decline (and I did begin to try that tack after a while, for my many goodly reasons), he did not like me to stay home without him. I could not ever talk him out of going altogether and so I tried to convince him that I did not always like to go with him. He quickly became angry with me when I did not want to do as he wished. Keeping my husband happy, particularly *with* me, was my paramount desire in the beginning of our marriage, and so I relented to many things that I somewhat regretted later on.

Before I had my children, and long before we eventually moved into his mother's house and town, when my husband used to take me to saloons with him, I grew to generally detest that world of men and women. Saloons were places where my husband seemed entirely comfortable, but I was mortified with the kinds of people and behavior that existed therein. To begin with, the air of most any saloon was thick with smoke which felt grievous uncomfortable to my lungs. From my experiences, the general atmosphere was horribly loud with shouting, swearing and insane laughter; and the behaviors of many folks there was vulgar to say the least. Beyond all that discomfort to my body and soul, the spirit of these places seemed to me to be very dark and low down.

When first I went to saloons with my husband, I had thought that he simply wanted his wife beside him to partake in a few drinks, and to be there to dance with him when any lively and inviting music played well enough to entice his feet to get up and move spritely. Let me in all fairness say, that there was some music that I did enjoy in several saloons. Energetic piano music tends to get my toes tapping and I do enjoy dancing. This was the only thing at a saloon that might ever call to me, and was one reason that I initially agreed to go to such establishments with my husband in the first place. I hoped to dance. I hoped to dance with my husband, and I expected that he would wish to dance with me. My expectations were lowered fairly quickly over time.

To my dismay, my husband danced with me very little, and less and less as time dragged onward. He preferred to dance with other young women. He adored the dancing girls. After dancing with these females, he would throw them and even worse women onto his lap all the while I sat there horrified nearby and wishing myself far away (and out of that situation which was excruciating to me).

He certainly wished to make me feel jealous of him and whatever female he threw about the dance floor with him or tossed onto his lap somewhere near where I was sitting, waiting. What cruelty for a husband to treat his wife in such a way. He seemed to delight in torturing me thusly. I was certain of that apparent fact. My husband had a cruel streak in him, at least where I was concerned, it seemed to me.

My husband also strangely became jealously guarded of me whenever any other man would begin to show me any attention.

At least my husband saved me from *that* sort of tiresome difficulty. I did not have to dance with or to shoo away any man that might make any advance towards me, because my husband would stop dancing or put any other woman aside to then come guard his property (as in myself). I was thankful to my husband for that at least. No, my dear reader, I did not like to regard myself as his property, and yes, I thought it dismally sad that the only way he would give me any due attention was when another man was interested my way. Yet, I was grateful that I did not end up having to deal with any crude advances from other men in those saloons, because my husband would not allow for such as that. At least his husbandry encompassed that protection for me.

I would sit at a table, as if alone in each saloon. I near always cringed at the experience. I did not belong in such a bawdy atmosphere. I felt as if a bird thrown down into mud, no longer flying but only mired in filth. My husband was of that lewd class of saloon people and I was of another kind of people, on another plane of existence. No, he had not been raised that way to become that type of man, at least not by his churchgoing mother. He had *become* what he was on his own. He had chosen that sort of lower life. He was a lewd man of his own making. I clearly saw that our morals were utterly opposing. And add to all that general discomfiture for me, as a poor wretched wife, I was forced to see, or at least to know, that my husband cavorted with women there in front of me, and in front of all those other folks who were in attendance at the saloons those nights. What entire embarrassment. What public humiliation. What inner heartbreak.

Later on I realized that what my husband did in front of me was only a hint of what he would do behind my back. Yes, if he would behave so inappropriately with other women, with me near and free to see him misbehaving, of course he would do more and worse when he was out cavorting and I was at home. Nonetheless, I came to choose to stay home (with my babies as my excuse) and to turn my back on whatever my husband chose to do with other women in or near saloons, or elsewhere. I saw no other choice to make. My husband's choices were his own and not under my control. I could only choose for myself, with proper regards to myself and my children.

19
His Sister

Gretchen was a gregarious spirit with an open temperament. She might have been a slight type of embarrassment to kin as reclusive as the Weiss family. This is what I tended to think when I first knew her at all, for her manner seemed so contrary to the reserved nature that Mr. and Mrs. Weiss and their musician upstairs exhibited. To my knowledge, or at least as I had gathered thus far, this Weiss family consisted of the parents, a son and a daughter; and now I knew of a certainty that Gretchen was the oldest child and only daughter.

Was Gretchen's sudden appearance, to the Weiss family's chagrin? I almost certainly surmised as much. At least at first I did. It all came out soon enough, though. When Gretchen arrived for a visit and began talking, at least a good deal of the mystery of the Weiss family musician began to unfold. She had been travelling abroad, or some such thing, as I first understood, but she was back with her family for a lengthy stay. Now a married Mrs. Gretchen Jennings, the Weiss parents' daughter and the musician's sister was a true beauty, I would surely say.

One day when I had just arrived to work for Mrs. Weiss, I was met by the daughter instead of the mother, "Hello, my dear. I am the lost child returned. My name is Gretchen. You are Isabelle, I presume. Oh, my gracious, but you are even more beautiful than my mother described to me."

I was taken aback a good deal, "Oh, yes, well, thank you."

Full of vibrant effervescence, she gently ushered me into the parlor, "Here we go, my dearest. Let us talk a while and get to know one another."

"Oh certainly, yes, but where is Mrs. Weiss?"

"Oh, she is just upstairs with my brother: having a little chat of this or that, you see. She'll be down shortly, I presume. She won't want me talking your ears off for too terribly long, that I can wager for certain."

I sat. I waited. And I smiled.

"Well, well. You seem to be my mother's right hand or at least her favorite helper when you are here. I understand that she would like you here in the house with her more than you are able to come. I fancy she would also like to trade you for me, as far as daughters go."

"Oh, no, that could not be so."

"Oh yes: I am not her cup of tea, you see. No matter. I am not bothered by such things at all. She is as she is, and I am as I am. We are so very different, but she understands you more than me, I think."

"That is not likely, surely?"

"Quite likely, actually; but don't trouble yourself a moment on my account, my dear Isabelle. I am not sad one whit. I have an adoring husband to console me if I ever felt ignored or slighted in the least by my mother, or my father when it comes to it. But I do know that they love me. They simply do not know what to make of me. They seldom know what to do with me. They never have, you see."

I did not know how to answer and so sat silent, trying to appear pleasant, at least.

Gretchen bubbled vibrantly, "My gracious, but she speaks so very highly of you. I could not wait to meet you. With such high praise from my mother, I knew that I would adore you instantly. But I have you at a disadvantage. I suspect that she hasn't breathed a word about me to you. Well, she doesn't show her cards much. Keeps all things close to herself, you see. And so, it is of no matter to me that she hasn't told you all about me."

"Well, she did mention you, once or twice, just recently."

"Did she indeed?! Well, that is surprising news to me. She mentioned me to you? How wonderful! What did she tell you?"

"Well, I think that she said you were her only daughter, her oldest child, and fairly recently married, and away on a lengthy voyage."

"Yes, yes, a honeymoon trip and then some. But now my husband is terribly caught up in some business and so I thought that I would get out of his way to come visit my long lost family."

I ventured, "Well, that is lovely that you can visit your family after all this time; though, I would think that you will miss your husband? And he you?"

Gretchen delighted, "Oh, yes. We are inseparable lovebirds; but with him being so busy with his work currently, I grabbed the opportunity to come out for a visit. I thought that we could do without each other this once, a little while. He could not come, I wanted to come, and so I flew the coop. I'm a flighty thing, a spontaneous sort, you see. Like a bird. Good thing my husband adores me."

I simply smiled.

"Well, and you sew for my mother as you keep her company?"

"Yes, mostly, you could say that. I am very grateful to her for the easy work, and good pay."

"From what she has told me, you are a perfect companion for her: a good listener and a pleasant and reserved young lady. I gather that you never vex her like I tend to do."

"I can't imagine you vexing her."

Gretchen laughed, and then continued, "Oh yes, I assure you that I do vex my mother quite often. I think that my endless chatter unnerves her somewhat. She is not unhappy with or ashamed of me, of course, but she does not like how indiscreet I can tend to be. I talk far too much, you see. I reveal too much. It is my inborn nature. I cannot help myself. Not at all, you see."

I only nodded, just a little, as I was trying not to smile too much.

"I think and I speak, plain and simple. In point of fact, I speak before thinking or I think aloud, or something of that nature. I cannot refrain from asking and telling all manner of things that I should not. My poor mother must suffer my impropriety."

"I can't imagine you being improper."

"Yes, well, I am terribly ill-mannered. My conduct is not measured in the least and my tongue is the quickest in the west, east and in-between you see."

I could not help but, "You seem a delightful companion to me, Gretchen. May I call you Gretchen? Or would you prefer that I call you by 'Mrs. Jennings'?"

"Oh no! Please! Do not call me 'Mrs. anything'. That seems so very dull to me. You will make me feel an old matron with that sort of speech. Yes, please do call me Gretchen. It sounded so very pleasant falling off of your lips. And so you find me *delightful*, do you? How gracious of you to think so nicely of me!"

"Not gracious at all: simply my honest observation."

"Well, I like honest. Even if I don't like what somebody has to say to me, I will take honest over a falsehood any day of the week. I abhor lies. Tell me you despise me if it is true and I will be content, but do not tell me you like me *just* to please me, for such as that will not please me at all."

"I like to be honest if I am given half the chance to do it. I dislike dishonesty as well. And there is room in the world for differences, I should say. But who could ever despise *you*, Gretchen?"

"You might be surprised, Isabelle. My husband's *mother*, for one."

"What? *Why*?"

"Well, likely only simply that she had another young lady in mind for him to marry. That is all as far as I can figure out."

"And she did not accept you as her son's wife, once you were married?"

"I doubt she will ever accept me. Yes, she does not like me and so I do not like her."

"I am sorry for that. I am sorry for you. I can only imagine."

"And *your* mother-in-law? Is she good to you?"

"Yes, *very*. But, more importantly, she is perfectly kind and loving to my children. *That* is the most important thing to me."

"Oh yes, certainly. I will hope for that."

"But it is sad that she will not like you."

"Well, it is of no account to me. At least I don't mind that she does not like me, as long as I am not left alone with her too very much. That is the greatest reason why I am here: to get away from her."

"Oh?"

"Yes, I did not like to be left alone to my husband's mother, particularly in my new condition."

I was intrigued, and could easily guess but asked instead, "Your condition?"

Gretchen was happy to begin to inform me, "Yes, to own the entire truth, I told my husband to bring me here for my confinement or I would get myself to the train on my own. And he knows I would have done it, rebellious creature that I am."

I then asked the obvious, "You are with child, then?"

She glowingly answered, "Oh yes, did I not already make that perfectly clear? Yes, we are overjoyed with the prospect of our very own baby. We cannot wait to hold our first child in our arms."

"Of course, but will you have your husband near when the joyous event finally takes place? Will he travel back here to be with you before your time of travail comes?"

"Yes, yes, I have commanded him to come a good while before I am due to deliver our earthly angel. I confess that *he* would rather that our baby be born in his mother's house, or our own home near to her, but *I* wished to be near my own mother for such an event and he complied with my need. He will be here for our first little miracle."

"And so you will enjoy the company of your family here in the meantime?"

Gretchen laughed a little before saying with a beaming smile,

"Oh, yes. *I* will enjoy myself greatly. The only question is this: will *they* be able to abide my being here for so very long?"

"Oh, Gretchen, I cannot imagine them not enjoying you being here. As I have already said, you are a delight, at least to my mind."

"Yes, well, I know that my parents and my brother do love me, but unfortunately, I am certain to embarrass them from time to time at least. I am an open book, I wear my heart on my sleeve, and I talk endlessly. These things about me are too much for *especially* my mother to bear sometimes; but if I keep to the house, and do not go out and talk to the neighbors or in the town much at all, I might make less of a nuisance of myself as far as my family is concerned."

Gretchen's brother began playing upstairs. I was happy to realize that it was my song that he played. My favorite song was floating in the air. I closed my eyes and was lost in it for only a second or two.

She spoke to end that magic in effect, "Oh my, but I *do* love that song. Well, now that he is playing, we can be assured that my mother will be here at any moment. I will hush myself and make her believe that I am being discreet."

My song was played by the musician, brother and son, as Gretchen and I both listened to it filling the house and likely round about. Though, perhaps I listened more intently than Gretchen. For at least a moment, I was quite lost in it.

20
My Guest

I was stunned to see Gretchen at the door for me and so I could not help but ask, "What are you doing here?"

She laughed and then smiled, "Oh, I am sorry to surprise you like this, but I wanted to talk to you, and I simply could not wait until you came back to work for my mother again."

"Oh, no, I mean, yes, that is just fine."

"I thought that we could be friends, or at least I wanted to be as your friend, and so here I am to call upon you. I hope I am not inconveniencing you."

"No, no, not at all. I will ask my mother-in-law if she can watch my children for me, or perhaps they could play near us. Would you like to sit in the parlor or take a turn around the yard, or sit outside or something?"

"Oh yes, we could walk or sit in the yard. I prefer the outdoors when the weather is fine. And since it was so very fine out today, I set out to find you."

"You walked all this way to see me?"

"You walk all that way to work for my mother."

"Yes, but your condition."

"Oh, I feel perfectly fine. I feel quite wonderful, in fact. I am over the worst stage, not feeling sick at all anymore, and yet I have not been burdened in size as yet."

"Yes, you look wonderful too. I am glad that you feel so very fine."

"Yes, I am thankful for it."

I held up a finger to beg a moment, called up to my children to come play outside, and then guided Gretchen towards the gardens furthest away from the house, beyond and towards the outer-most parts of the property. I wanted some privacy in case the elder Mrs. Ramstock might be tempted to listen in on our conversation, not that she was anything close to a busybody or gossip, you understand. I was not in the habit of ever having any guests over and I did not like to think that my new friend and I would have to moderate our speech in any way in order not to be overheard.

There was a lovely bench off and away that seemed perfect for the purpose. As little Lorna and Alan caught up with and joined us, I introduced Gretchen to my children before we all trundled to that outlying part of the Ramstock property.

I pointed to my favorite bench in the place, "Sit now, Gretchen. You must be tired from your long walk."

"Not at all, not really, but I will sit. My feet might appreciate that from me by now."

"There, are you comfortable enough? Do please let me know if you would like water or any kind of refreshment. I can send my children in to get something. They would love to serve us."

"Oh, yes, perhaps in a few moments, but not just yet. In passing, I begged a little water from a neighbor not far from here, and she gave me some cookies as well. Very obliging. Very neighborly. Mrs. Manson. Do you know her very well?"

"Yes, she is a lovely woman. Seven daughters, did you know? And several sons as well. Is that not an amazing thing? I can only imagine having so many children. Did she tell you about all of her children?"

Gretchen laughed aloud. "Yes! I think I was introduced to the lot of them!"

"They are quite a wonderful family. And her husband seems a gem too."

Gretchen settled into her spot on the seat and then turned full towards me, as if intent on something, "And so, my friend… may I call you my *friend*, Isabelle?"

I smiled. "Of course you may."

"Well, this is a very fine thing: visiting my dearest friend in her lovely garden."

I only smiled.

"Your children are quite darling. And so quiet, for children, I should say."

"Yes, they are both very good-natured. I cannot claim all responsibility for their good behavior, though. Their grandmother deserves a good deal of the credit, since she commandeers them so very much for me."

"Oh yes, that is a very fine thing for you. I am glad for you. Well, well. And so my mother is very happy that I have chosen to make you my best friend around here."

I did not know what to say in response and so only said, "Oh."

"Yes, she trusts you and would rather I spout off about anything to you instead of who knows who in the town."

I laughed. I couldn't help myself. I thought her comment funny in a way.

She laughed as well. "Yes, I've told you how indiscreet and chatty I naturally am and you know how my mother wants all our family secrets kept quiet, even in the house. But I am always about to burst out loud about everything, and so it would not do for me to talk to anyone but *you*."

"You can always talk to me, and any secret you might ever tell me, will always be perfectly safe with me."

"Oh yes, I know it. My mother quite assured me of the safety of talking to you. I know she hasn't told you much of anything because it is her way to hold things in, or to keep most everything close to her vest so to speak, but as she and I both know: I am a horrid secret-keeper. And so, here I am, living in this town a good while, trying to bite my tongue and to keep the family laundry hidden whenever I talk to anyone around here."

I simply smiled.

"In a large city, you know, one can always find a stranger to tell all that is on your mind. You see, somehow a stranger feels safe to confide anything in, because you will likely never see them again. And if you do happen to see them, well, you are strangers and likely won't even remember your former meeting."

I took her word for that which I had never experienced, "I suppose so."

Gretchen carried on, "And it is in my nature to get out, talk round about, chat a good deal, and make friends and all that sort of thing. I tend to hate to be cooped up and silent. It suits my parents and my brother, for they like to remain in the home and quiet; well, save for my brother's constant piano playing. You know what I mean, I dare say. You know us, or at least them, my family; enough to know what I am saying."

"Yes, I think that I do."

Gretchen breathed in deeply and looked around the yard. "What a fine day it is. Do not you think so?"

"Most certainly, I am very glad to be out enjoying it."

"And not working."

"Yes."

"I mean for other people."

"Yes, of course."

She cast me a glance of apparent compassionate concern, "Not cooped up with my mother."

"Well, on days that I work for her, I enjoy my walk to and fro, and I also enjoy your mother's company. She is always very kind to me. Working for her is not truly like work. It is more like an enjoyment."

"That comforts me to know. Well, I would not fear otherwise, I suppose."

"And, I will confide, most truthfully, that I thoroughly enjoy the music there. Working in your parent's house is sometimes somewhat like going to a concert, and sitting afar off from the stage."

Gretchen chuckled. "Oh, yes. I see what you mean. I suppose some people would find the music too much, on occasion, but if one enjoys such piano playing, as I do myself as well, then, yes, entering the Weiss home is like going back stage to a concert of sorts."

"I certainly would say that it is."

"Or like being down in the orchestra pits, perhaps?"

"Well, the music does emanate from above while one sits beneath it. I prefer to think of it as if it were Heavenly music falling from above." I smiled.

"Oh Isabelle, what a *lovely* way to think of my brother's music."

21
Frederick

Speaking of Frederick, my brother, you know, I wanted to talk to you about him."

I had not known that the musician's name was Frederick as yet. Frederick Weiss. I thought his name had a nice ring to it. I suddenly wondered what he looked like, more than I had ever been tempted to before. I had seen him from afar momentarily each time, but only from too far away to be able to make a proper judgment. I still wondered about him on occasion, without really wanting to, without trying, without thinking. I could not help it.

I feigned away from my former ignorance of Gretchen's brother's name, "Frederick? Yes?"

"Well, my dear Isabelle, I think that he is doing better these days: a little better, at least in a few ways."

"Better?"

"Yes, well, I suppose my mother has told you nothing of him."

"No, not at all."

"Not at all then?"

"Not one whit. She does not speak of him to me. She never has."

"Oh my gracious. Never?"

"Never."

"She has told you *nothing* of him?"

"Nothing, no, to my recollection, she has never mentioned him in *any* way. I am quite certain of it. She avoids the subject of who plays the piano upstairs. In fact, it is as if there is no music playing in her house at all."

"Oh, my gracious. Indeed. That must seem so very strange to you, and to all around, I wager. No *wonder* people have been speculating. Well, that is her secretive way. *I* would be explaining *everything* to everyone. Well, perhaps not. Perhaps I would not explain quite every little detail to every person. My brother would not like that. No, he would not like that at all."

I tried to be helpful, "I suppose one could strike a balance between telling a little something to someone, without telling too much for the family's comfort."

"Oh yes, though my comfort and my parents' and brother's comforts are two very different things, you see. I would be happy to lay almost everything out for all to see. It is only the fact that I wish to respect my family's wishes and to be sensitive to my brother's feelings that I will only tell a very few details to, well, to someone such as *you*."

I tried to nod comfortingly and respectfully. I did not wish to encourage her to tell more than she should, nor to suggest by my looks, behavior or speech, that I was any sort of gossip intent on finding anything or everything out. Of course, I was *curious*. I had long wondered; but I was not the busybody type. I know myself well enough to at least claim that.

"Well, back to my brother Frederick." she said.

"Yes, Frederick. Yes?" I tried not to appear biting at the bit.

She continued, "And so my mother has not even hinted of his tragic history?"

"Tragic history? No, though I did imagine there must have been *something*, but I did not like to listen to the speculative talk around town."

"Oh yes, there would have been a good deal of talk and speculation. My mother has known of or at least suspected rumors, some silly or quite wild, I dare say. Well, anyway, I could make you guess as to what I allude to in the way of my brother's past, but that would be cruel at most or a stupid game in the least, so I will simply *tell* you outright."

I waited with bated breath. How long had I wondered about the musician and what had brought him to the point of hiding away upstairs and playing so many hours of his days and even into his nights like that? Would I now finally hear all about him and what had caused his heartache or other injury? Would I learn of his eccentricity?

She dug in with the beginnings of her brother's history, "So, you see my dear Isabelle, my father had come into a good deal of extra money through a sudden, surprising and lucky inheritance, and thus my parents had decided that we were all doing a grand tour of Europe. My parents also thought that Frederick could benefit from the masters: his music, you know. He wanted to meet other musicians and composers. He wanted to learn from any master who would teach him anything at all. My father could certainly afford some lessons for Frederick now. And so, we went."

I sat, listening intently to Gretchen's story, whilst my children played a little way off (but still within my tangential hearing). I looked over at the house briefly, wondering if my mother-in-law was curious as to my visitor and our conversation. Not that the elder Mrs. Ramstock was a snoopy sort of woman. Not at all, I assure you.

My visitor leaned in closer to me as she quietly shared, "Frederick saw many masters play at concerts and he was able to meet a few. For the passion of his music, he was determined to overcome his great inborn reserve enough to go before any of those grand musicians. He listened, he watched, he learned from them and he even played for them. You understand, my dear Isabelle, he could and can but listen even once and then play an exact copy of whatever he hears. It is an amazing genius he was born with, you see. He also creates many of his own tunes, of course, and he always has done, since he was a little boy."

I could not but interject, somewhat passionately and even at some length, "Oh, Gretchen, please do forgive me for my interruption, but I cannot call them simply *tunes*. Some could call them tunes, and perhaps they are tunes to you, but I cannot truly say tunes are what your brother plays. The word 'tunes' seems far too trivial a term to me. I would call all that I have ever heard Frederick play, true masterpieces. Anything that your brother plays seems astoundingly grand to me. Whether of his own creation or a copy of one of the master musicians in Europe, I cannot say that whatever he plays is anything less than genius. Once again, I apologize for appearing rude with my long-winded interjection. I am certain that I am very ignorant about these higher things of music, but I like to be entirely honest. I simply could let that moment pass without saying what I thought of your brother's playing. I only cannot think of his music as tunes, you see."

She smiled. "Oh no, not at all, Isabelle, I thoroughly agree with you. Frederick does *not* play tunes. He does certainly play and compose masterpieces, just as you have so accurately stated."

I smiled in return and then let my face show her with inquisitiveness that I was waiting for a continuation in Frederick's story.

Gretchen continued further, "We were all having a fairly delightful time. Frederick was in his element. He was gaining in confidence, learning much, and being given a good deal of accolades. In fact, he performed in some impressive places to important people."

'Yes, and?' I thought as I sat silently.

"And then, there she was: that *woman*. She was beautiful, I grant you; but she was an artful thing and I could see her manipulations right off. My mother did not like her for the same and similar reasons as I. My father could see no fault in her in the beginning. Men aren't always entirely astute to these things where women are concerned, as I am certain that you well know. Perhaps only a woman can truly recognize the depraved depths of a conniving female. I am sorry to say it, but Frederick was flattered, enraptured, captivated and fooled, through and through."

I was certain that my eyes had widened. All I offered was, "Oh."

"My mother and I even went so far as to have some serious

conversations with each other and then tried to warn Frederick together. We thought that the young woman was at least after some money, from our family, you know, and of course, Frederick was in a fast way of becoming the toast of Europe with his piano playing and composing. That wicked conniving woman obviously wanted to be a part of all of that. Sadly, my brother would not listen to us and threw himself out in front to defend her from us. My father was no help. He simply told us to give Frederick our blessings that he would be happy with his choice. And so, Frederick married her."

I wanted to guess that she turned out to be everything horrid that they suspected. I was certain of that. I was sitting on the edge of the bench, all attention, waiting to hear the end of the story. And then my children suddenly ran up to show us some interesting sticks that they had found.

I felt obliged to pay my children a little attention, "Oh, my. Those are quite different looking sticks."

Lorna and Alan each said their little piece about their natural treasures and then I suggested that they go inside and ask their grandmother for a little refreshment and gave them permission to bring any little thing out to my guest and I, if they liked, and if their grandmother was so inclined to give them something to share with us. I thought that my sudden suggestion might buy me enough time to hear the rest of Gretchen's story about her brother Frederick. I turned my attention back to her as my children ran off towards the house.

She breathed in deeply before saying more, "Well, we all hoped and prayed that all would turn out well in spite of our worries, especially my mother and I, you see; but *that* woman ensnared my brother in her web and drained him of all his energy and time. She kept him from his music. He composed nothing. He didn't even play. She kept him from his family. She kept him from everything. She caused him to entirely revolve around her continual whims. She spent all his money and then sent him to my father to get more, over and over again. And then, when my father began to object to supporting such things, she was off."

"Off?"

"Yes, she ran off. We found out in due time that she ran off and away with another man."

I was certainly shocked. "Oh, my goodness!"

"Yes."

I begged to know more, "And what then? Did she turn up again? Did she come back? Did Frederick search for her? Did you all hear of her? Is there more to this story?"

"Frederick was broken-hearted, of course."

"But did she come back?"

"No."

"Did he search for her?"

"At first I thought that he might, but, no, he did not. He only kept to his room. He would not like anyone to think so, but I do think that he spent at least many days of weeping."

"So, she *never* came back? He never saw her again?"

"No."

"And so, he is still married to her, then?"

"Oh, no. Because of abandonment and adultery, which my father was able to gather enough evidence and proof for, a bill of divorcement was granted before we came home to America."

"Well, I should say that a divorce is far better than not, in such a case as his. That is very lucky that he was able to get one."

Gretchen was as serious as I had ever seen her thus far, "Yes, we are all very thankful that a divorce was possible in Frederick's circumstance."

"But, he is still broken-hearted over her?"

"Well, I would not necessarily say that. Frederick *was* extremely confused as well as heartbroken for a while."

"Oh, I had generally thought that he kept to his room because he was heartbroken. Some of the music that he plays seems to evoke the pain of the heart."

"Yes, he is wont to be playing melancholy tunes a good deal too much."

"I have seemed to notice that when he plays the *violin*, there is more melancholy spirit present than usual."

She agreed, "Oh yes, I think I could say that the violin is his instrument of woe."

"And so you do not think that he laments the loss of her? His wife, I mean?"

"Oh no, I think that his heart has healed for the most part by now. It is not really that. I know that he feels ashamed that he has been divorced. He feels stupid that he was fooled by her. He would wish to go back and try again, you see. I mean that he would rather that he had never married her at all, of course. Frederick thinks that good people will think ill of him when they find out that he is divorced."

"Oh, but he is faultless. All the sins lie at his former wife's feet."

"Oh yes, I agree with you entirely. But, he is so very hard on himself and is inclined to think that he has not a friend in the world. Frederick would never think this, and I know that I am wicked for saying it, but it would have been better for my brother had his wife simply died."

"Or that he had never met her."

"Well, yes, that would have been for the best."

"I can completely understand your point of view and sentiments, but surely Frederick has learned a great deal through his experience in life? There is always a silver lining to every cloud, is there not? I would hope so."

"We can hope, but we cannot see Frederick's silver from his dark cloud just yet."

"He is young, he is talented, and I venture he must be somewhat handsome? I would think that he could marry again in the near future?"

"As his sister, I should say that he is indeed very handsome, but I am biased in my opinion, of course. Well, we can think and hope that he will marry and settle happily in due time, but he seems to have no intention of ever marrying again. He seems to have chosen to remain monkish. He has not trusted his ability to judge a person's character ever since his ill-fated marriage. He fears he would make a bad choice in a wife, again. Besides, he does not think any good woman would want to marry him now. He imagines himself a tainted man."

"Give him time, Gretchen. He will rally, he will realize he has gained wisdom, and he will find that many a good woman would be willing to marry him, I am certain."

She smiled. "Yes, you must be right."

22
Sunsets

If not for Mrs. Ramstock wishing me to go to church with her and my children, I think that I can say in all honesty that I might not have gone at all. Certainly I would not have gone nearly so often. I had grown up mostly going to church each Sunday. I had always thought that I would go to church weekly. Churchgoing had always been a part of my life, you see. But when my unhappiness with my husband gradually dawned on me, my faith in anything began to fade away. As I lost general faith in marriage because of my horrid husband, I also lost faith in most everything else. Yes, I was become as a lost soul so to speak.

I felt forsaken and so in a sort of natural consequence way, I began to forsake my former beliefs. For perhaps a few years, my heart had not been forged in any religion or perhaps in any belief of higher beings and places. I suppose I had stopped praying altogether, at least from the inner depths of my heart. What had heartfelt praying got me after all? Only really tears. Or at least so it seemed to me. I felt alone, lost, forgotten. Where was Heaven for me? My heart and thoughts were only for my children. I was a mother who loved her children, and that was about all. I had all but given up on my childhood and youthful Godly beliefs until that day I first heard the musician play. My soul was captured. My spirit was lifted. I believed again. My heart was filled.

Do not misunderstand me. I do not mean to say that my heart had been taken by the musician, the man, for I had not yet seen him; and indeed, since I had thought the musician *either* woman or man, *that* material point did not matter one jot to me. It was the music that awoke and raised my spirit. It was the Heavenly quality of soul of the pianist whom I had been drawn to, as if a true eternal sister or brother: a kindred spirit. My feelings for the musician were on a higher spiritual plain than that of earthly attractions. I appreciated the divineness of the gift: I recognized the divinity in that music. Whatever might be still angelic within me was awoken by those songs.

My deadened soul was resurrected by the Heavenly music to live again, and so I could not but feel gratitude to the musician who played. I felt a grateful kind of love for this pianist before I could imagine who she or he might be, or what they might look like. Of these material things I did not care. Not knowing that the musician was a man, and indeed, somewhat hoping and imagining that the musician was actually a woman; freed me to think and feel all the more warmly towards that pianist.

Whether the musician was man or women had been of no real regard to me, as I say. At first I did not think upon the general ramifications to me if the pianist turned out to be a man. I could not imagine myself tempted to think or even feel beyond my marriage promises. I never had been tempted. Not a once. No matter how my husband broke his marital vows with me, I always stayed fully true to my own vows with my God. Even when I doubted God's existence, I still would not betray my marriage promises. Yes, I have always been true to my own marriage vows notwithstanding being yoked to a brute that continually has broken his promises to me.

Nonetheless, I know that no man or woman is truly above enticements of this world. As much as I might think myself beyond temptation, I know myself to be human. I know that our societal morals and the bounds of propriety between men and women are set down as a protection for us all. These precautions are a necessity to any decent person. Certain rules of society maintain the morals of the people within it.

We can each possibly become persuaded to do wrong. We each

must take care. We must step around the traps of this world. Every one of us could fall into a pit if we did not step carefully around it. And we cannot walk into or near any fire without getting at least tinged by the flames.

And so, though my inner spirit self was deeply spoken to by the notes, the melody, and the harmony, and I was transfixed by the formula of the music, I could not allow myself to cross over into any precarious territory of being intrigued by the man who played that music. I knew that I must draw a line that I would not cross. I should not ever dare think on Frederick, the man.

Beyond the musician, the man, I always focused on the music that was played. I saw the melodiousness as a gift from Heaven. I looked upward to where it was sparked from. I separated the divine blessing from its earthly giver. I bonded to the music itself.

Yet, I still digress, dear reader. I mean to mention more of my reawakened spirit and the rebirth of my faith due to the music. I wish to share how the musician's talent and skill brought me back into God's fold, in a way.

When I have spoken of my lost faith in Heavenly things because of the hellish experiences I suffered under due to my horrid husband, I am certain that some would say to me that the heavenly glories on earth should have sufficed enough to keep me firmly bonded to my beliefs. Sunsets, sunrises, clouds, rainbows, trees, flowering fields: all these things of God's creations should have been enough to keep me believing in God. Simply the growing grass at my feet should have been enough. Yes, I can fully agree in principle.

The world around us is always full of Heavenly reminders. Even or perhaps especially my angelic children should have been enough to speak to and remind me of Heaven. Perhaps God's imprint in the world around us is enough for some people who are stronger in their faith than I was. But you see, my dear reader, for me, weighed down and under by the relatively recent events of my own life, events that seemed lodged in time as if miserably forever, I grew weary of holding onto hopes of things of a better. I could not seem to hold myself up. I was drowning in desolation and so could not see above the darkened sea that I had been pulled under.

And so, the musician came to town and played, and his music lifted me. In its way, the music saved me. It pulled me up and out of my drowning state of despair. It awoke me. I began to truly live again. Beyond being mother to my children, in and of myself, I felt a woman, a person, a living human being once more. The world around me brightened.

Suffice it to say that I am mesmerized and transported Heavenward whenever I hear the musician play. I say heavenward, dear reader, because I think that I truly do believe in Heaven once again. It seems years since I have had much of any ability in holding to faith.

Being innocently naive as well as powerless to choose anything else for myself, I had married badly, unknowingly. And then I was forced to live in a nightmarish world; but now sunlit dreams beckon me to walk past that Tudor house and hear the musician playing. Frederick's music calls to me.

My husband likely does not imagine what is in my mind and heart about many things. I tell him truly nothing. I never really have. We always were as strangers. My thoughts and feelings have never been safe with my husband, and so I quickly learned to keep all to myself. And thus, I live in my own type of Hell, still, while I sometimes dream of Heaven. Neither even sunsets nor my children were enough to keep my faith alive as it should have been, but it was the music that finally renewed my beliefs.

23
Mr. Weiss, the Elder

He never spoke to me except to say a 'hello' in passing. It was not that the elder Mr. Weiss was aloofly rude, but he obviously preferred to leave me to his wife and to only speak to her. I soon noticed that he was that way with any woman who worked for his wife. He did not tend to speak to any female in the house except for his wife and daughter. He left women workers to them. He was reserved with other women.

Mr. Weiss, the elder, was the same way at church. He was reticent with women other than in his immediate family, though, he was far more communicative with the men. Don't misunderstand me in thinking that he had a gregarious way, for he did not, but he seemed far more comfortable in talking to other men than to women.

Now, I do not say that Mr. and Mrs. Weiss attended the town church weekly, for they didn't tend to. Indeed, they had waited a great stretch of time before first attending at all. And then, they did not come as often as some might have wished of them. Although they did not come every week, they did come with a certain regularity. I had long since noticed that there were those families or folks in the congregation who went to church most every week, rain or shine, snow or no; and then there were those who came every two or few weeks. Of course, there were also those people who came to Sabbath worship very rarely, such as only for Christmastime and Easter.

My mother Ramstock liked me to go to church with her and

my children every week and I did try to oblige her wishes. Without the elder Mrs. Ramstock plodding me on, I might have been far more likely to go far less often. Her husband, however, chose not to go to church with his wife, except for Christmas and Easter and once or twice in-between. I had no quarrel with my father-in-law over that detail. I only noticed it.

I did like to see that Mr. and Mrs. Weiss tended to go to church together almost always. If she did not attend, he did not either. And she did not seem to like to go without him. They sat together, stood together, and seemed quite happily together as an old married pair. Yes, it was true that there were moments when Mrs. Weiss would stand off a little way to talk to a lady friend, and Mr. Weiss with any man he might choose to speak to. You see, my dear reader, there was this essence of their togetherness that I hint at. I liked to see it.

As I have alluded to, it was not that Mr. Weiss was not a talker at all. No, I heard him converse quite adeptly with the men who worked for him (and, as I have suggested, I had seen him speaking with other men somewhat at church), with his wife and daughter, and also with his son upstairs. Yes, I sometimes heard the Weiss father and son talking. I could not decipher what they said to each other, not that I actually tried to comprehend (not wanting to eavesdrop), but I could hear the sense of conversations, sometimes lively and other times calm. Their tones of voice and the spirit of any banter between them did carry downstairs. And though I thought that there was an occasional debate between the two, I would not say that there ever was any overriding anger or argumentative contention.

Indeed, from what I had noticed, I thought that at least the older Mr. Weiss and quite as likely the younger Mr. Weiss were even-tempered men. Anger was not their usual fare. I sensed a great difference there, as compared to two other men that I unfortunately knew too well. Mr. Ramstock the elder was far too much like my husband, having a sudden temper and tending towards arguments for little reason at all.

The contrast between Mr. Weiss, the elder, and Mr. Ramstock, the elder, was more and more evident to me. What I noticed most was perhaps mainly in the way that they each treated their wives. Mrs. Weiss was a cherished queen in her house. She could do no wrong in her husband's eyes. From what I could see, he was her fierce protector and defender. He would not allow any criticism of his wife, or at least this is what I had come to believe over time from what I did see and hear. I found this trait or tendency utterly charming.

Mr. Weiss seemed to adore his wife. I was certain that there was a firm bond between the two of them. Perhaps it was his choice from the beginning of their marriage to guard his beloved mate, or maybe he had learned over time through experience that it was a necessary and goodly thing.

Rather than being appreciated and shielded as she should have been, the elder Mrs. Ramstock was forced to play peacemaker frequently as she tried to appease and please her husband. He tended towards an ill temper oftentimes. I sometimes imagined that my mother-in-law might have been as happy to have her husband away as I was when her son was gone off. I did not think that her husband was as bad as mine, but I did not know beyond what I could see on the surface. At least my father-in-law put a handsome roof over his wife's head and I knew that she had her fair share of money to spend. My husband had never tended *that* way. And this was why I worked: to put away a few coins and to pay my way where I felt it necessary, as well as to dress myself decently (how could I sell my ability to sew if I was dressed always in rags?) and things of that nature. I did not want to be a charity case, even to my husband's mother.

In observing the elder Mr. Weiss somewhat from afar, not only did I compare him to my husband's father, but also to my own father. I began to look back to my childhood and upon how my father had treated my mother. As a child, I had not noticed many things amiss, but as a grown woman with a husband and children of my own, I could look back and begin to see the sad parallels.

I cannot say that my father was ever as wicked as my husband
has turned out to be, but I can say that I went from one evil to
another when I left my childhood home to marry. Perhaps I went
from a lesser evil to a worse one. But you see, in his way, my father
prepared me for this life of misery. In a large measure, he laid the
foundation that caused me to fall into this miserable life. Of course,
the bulk of the blame still belongs only at my husband's feet.

Mr. Weiss, and how he treated his family, was one of the people
along the way who inadvertently helped me to see from whence I
had come. To see a good and happy relationship between a man
and his wife is as if to shine a light into the dark to show what is
wrong elsewhere. Yes, I suppose I married to escape my father, in
part, only to find myself in a far fierier pit and place of pain and
suffering than what I was jumping out of. If I had only known to
where I was leaping, I should never have done it. But then, would
I have my children? I could never regret my children. I could not
allow myself to look back too much, but to only try to look forward
for my children's sake, and to try to help them choose better than I.

Of all the men that I had known thus far throughout my life,
I would wish for my son to turn out more like a Weiss man and
my daughter to marry a man such as that, than Alan to emulate his
own father or Lorna to marry the likes of a Ramstock. Yes, a gentle
man was to be far preferred, and to my comprehension, there was
nothing amiss in a quiet man.

I often thought about the elder and the younger men in
the Weiss household, and their relationship to each other. The
musician's father provided all for him whilst he played his music.
This seemed to illustrate to me the love of the father for his son.
Yes, some people would say that this was an indulgence or a type of
spoiling, but I thought of the instinct of a loving parent to protect
their child, no matter what all their ages. Between Father and
Mother Weiss, every request of the musician seemed to be taken
care of without any begrudging in the least. Frederick Weiss needed
to play his music, and his parents availed the place and the means
for him to do so. As provider of the feast so to speak, Mr. Weiss had

my greatest respect. I could have liked to thank him also for the music that I so enjoyed.

24
Reading

Mrs. Weiss smiled. "No sewing today my dear Isabelle. Would you read to me instead?"

"Yes, of course."

"I would like to close my eyes and only listen. I used to be a great reader, but in recent years I have found it tiring to read so very much. The thought just occurred to me this morning that you could read some of my favorite old books to me. That would be infinitely more satisfying to me than anything else you could do for me at present."

"Yes certainly, but Mrs. Weiss, there is something I wished to ask you. I've also been thinking this morning that perhaps you don't need me coming so very much, or maybe perhaps even at all, you know, since your daughter Gretchen is here for an extended visit? I almost feel dishonest taking your money in this way. Such as reading is not work, truly."

"Nonsense, I would not even think of asking you to read for me as a neighbor or other visitor. By paying you, I can feel free to impose upon you in a way that I would never do to a guest. I could not in good conscience ask Gretchen to read extendedly to me for free. No, I am very happy to pay you to read to me, if you are happy to make a little money doing it for me."

"Well, yes, of course. When you put it in that way, and if you wish; how can I argue with your sensible line of reasoning?"

She got up and started touching books on a shelf, "Let me see, what shall I have you read to me?"

I sat waiting for my assignment, easily patient, happily listening to the delightful music that I could hear being played upstairs.

Her back to me a short while, she then spoke in a way that seemed all of a sudden, as she seemed to be aimlessly moving books around, "You and he have lived parallel melancholy tunes, I tend to think."

I was more than just a little incredulous at her unexpectedly abrupt remark and so I thought aloud with my wondering, "Who?"

She replied with only this, "You and he have suffered similarly."

Again I queried, "Who?"

Her final answer shocked me, "My son: my only beloved son."

I pronounced his name in astonishment, "Frederick?"

She simply said, "Yes."

I did not know what to say in return and so sat silently.

"Gretchen is upstairs playing duets with Frederick."

I did my utmost to compose myself to say, "Oh, I did not know that Gretchen also played."

"Yes, she plays quite well. She is not a genius at the piano like her brother, but she has a vast deal of talent to call her own. Yes, I do think that she could hold her own up against most anyone who plays that instrument, except for the truly exceptional. And so, Gretchen told me that she gave you an idea of Frederick's sad marriage and divorce."

"Yes, it is all very sad."

"I am glad that she has chosen to tell you, and *only* you."

I thought that I should promptly reassure my dear employer, "And I will not tell *anyone* else, you can be assured of that."

Her back was still turned towards me, "I *knew* that you could be fully depended upon to be entirely prudent with those facts."

"Yes, of course I will."

"You have become almost like one of our family."

"Thank you. I very much enjoy our visits. And I have thoroughly enjoyed getting to know Gretchen as well. She is delightful."

"Gretchen adores you."

"I like her very much as well. Who could not like her? She is in a fair way to become the best friend that I have ever known."

"I like to think of you both as secure in a lasting friendship."

"I am certain we will remain good friends always."

"Gretchen has always been quick to make friends, but I've long told her that a few true friends are more worth the earning than a world of flighty ones."

I offered in agreement, "Oh yes, most assuredly."

"She and her brother have always been good friends to each other."

"They are lucky to have each other in that way. The music upstairs sounds very joyous."

"Gretchen always does Frederick a great deal of good when she is around."

"I can well imagine. She is all effervescence."

"He is quite happy when she is up there with him."

"That is as it should be."

Mrs. Weiss seemed to look a little wistful or listless from where I sat. She did not speak for that lengthy moment. There was a still sadness about her.

I thought to think forward or to inquire in a way, "I never see Frederick at church with you all."

"He will come eventually."

"Yes, of course, I was hoping so."

Mrs. Weiss sat down with her chosen book. I waited for her to hand it to me. She held fast to it, staring at it, "I don't wish to pry, Isabelle, but I cannot resist saying something to you."

"Yes?"

"Your husband is not much of a husband to you, is he?"

"He is gone a great deal."

"Like his father."

"Yes, and perhaps worse."

"Like Frederick's past wife."

"Yes, at least."

She looked at me somberly, with salted water fully welling in her eyes. My own tears were forced to follow.

At length we both composed ourselves, and then I began to read her book to her. I did my utmost to do an entertaining job of it. I gave my best interesting attempt at a type of theatrical reading to honestly earn the money that I knew Mrs. Weiss would insist on paying me, even if I were to resist or argue the matter. I thought that I had read quite well, and the lively music upstairs as a backdrop did my reading no harm at all.

25
Teatime

Gretchen met me as I came in and then she promptly took me into their parlor. After seating us both down, she announced, "My mother is not feeling well today. She asked *me* to take up your time."

"But, shall I not go, then? You need not visit with me. Your mother is ill. Perhaps you should attend to her needs. I can certainly return back home directly."

"No, no. I *ache* for female company. And anyway, my mother is sleeping at present. She only wants for some sleep I think. She does not always sleep that well at night."

"But I cannot take *payment* for visiting you, surely. I hope that your mother did not think of paying me today."

"Yes, yes: she would not bring you over and not pay you."

"But I am not *working* for her. Indeed, she hardly makes use of me anymore. I wonder that she wants to pay me to visit with and read to her."

"Well, we are not opposed to taking some free visits from you from time to time (at least I am not), but when you are at our beck and call, you shall be paid."

"But what will you have me do for you today?"

"I shall ring for tea things and you will serve us."

I laughed, "That is hardly *work*, Gretchen. How can I take payment for *that*?"

"Oh, please *hush* about it now. I want to pay you. My mother instructed me to do so. And if you will not take coin from me today, we will have to give more or something else later to make up for it."

"But, Gretchen, how can I feel good with myself if I am taking advantage of your mother in this way?"

"Enough. Let us talk no more of money. It is time for a tray of nourishment."

She rang the bell and asked, "Are you hungry?"

"Not terribly, actually, for I ate before I came over."

Her eyebrows rose up, and there was a teasing look in her eyes, "Well, I have ordered up some very tempting pastries and other things that you will surely want to try once you set your eyes upon them!"

I smiled. "Now that you mention it, I didn't eat so very much before I left, after all."

She laughed.

We talked a short while of light and almost superficial things, until the Weiss maid brought the tray.

As I poured our tea out for the two of us, I could not help but observe, "This is such a lovely tea set. What fine porcelain. Oh my, and with so much gilding, I hardly dare drink from these cups!"

"Yes, will you not feel like a princess or a queen drinking from these cups and nibbling from these little plates? It is a glorious service."

I put the pot down, "Oh yes, but you know, I have long been fond of teapots. It's the shape of them somehow. I know that they come in many varied shapes, but there is something about most teapots that speak to me in their own special way. Even the simple old brown clay teapots are a treasure to me."

In her jolly way, Gretchen claimed, "Short and round like myself, I dare say."

I laughed and corrected her to a degree, "You have a very good reason for becoming rounder, my dearest little mother-to-be!"

Gretchen giggled and added, "Come to think of it, I fancy that I look a little more like a coffee pot at this point. You, know, a slight essence of once having been tall and thinner, with a rounding protrusion changing the memory of how I looked before."

"It is only for a brief moment in greater time, dear Gretchen, and the reward is worth every discomfort, pain, and inconvenience, I assure you. There is nothing quite like becoming a mother."

Without really thinking to whom she was talking she instinctively stated, "Like becoming a wife."

I was without speech momentarily. I wasn't sure as yet what was best for me to say in return.

Suddenly far more serious than her usual self, she quickly realized her possible blunder and attempted recovery, "I am one of the lucky women, through no special deserving of my own. My husband is a wonderful fellow. Please forgive me for being so insensitive to your plight, Isabelle. I can only wish that you were so very blessed as you should have been."

I did not want Gretchen to feel badly for speaking as she had and so I tried to cheer her up by saying, "Well, I am very blessed where my children are concerned, and my mother-in-law is better than most, I wager. We must always count our blessings to see how they outshine our cursings. You see, the silver lining in the dark grey cloud of my marriage is that my husband is usually gone away bothering other women instead of me."

Gretchen didn't laugh as I was trying to bring about. My silly attempt at a joke had been too sad a one. It was too true and terrible a general subject to be humorous, I supposed. I tried again, on another tack, "Gretchen, you certainly do deserve a good husband. All good women do. And, by the same token, all good men deserve a good wife. Sometimes some people are simply unlucky in love, I suppose. I dare say that I am a good enough woman to deserve a good husband. It is only an unlucky happenstance that I got a bad one. No, you know what? He could have been a good husband. He chose to be otherwise. His mother taught him the best that she could, she loved him, she set him a good example, and then along the way, he chose to follow more in his father's footsteps, and I fear a good deal further in a very bad direction. My husband chose the path that he now walks on, every step of the way. He is what he wants to be. He chooses his sins, one at a time."

Gretchen could not smile, but only said, "I suppose so, but I am still so very sorry for what you must live with."

"Well, I have my children. They are everything to me. And, you know, what if my husband had been wonderful to me and then died? I would be in very much the same position now. I keep telling myself *that* and it does help me to feel somewhat better. And, what if I did not have my mother-in-law to support me and to help me raise my children so nicely? Where would I be then? Much worse off. Likely even horribly destitute. No, I prefer to count my blessings."

"Yes, but if your husband had died, you could marry again. You are still young and beautiful. As it is, you cannot marry again."

"If my husband had been wonderful and had died, I would more than likely *not* wish to marry again, I should think. My husband is as if no husband at all, and I *cannot* marry again. I know the two circumstances are very different, but they are similar in their ways, and if I look at my situation in a certain way, it does not seem so very bad. Besides, if I were suddenly free to marry again, I do not think I would wish to consider it anyway."

"Why ever not?"

"Because of fear: I would be afraid that I would make a bad choice all over again. I did not choose well back then. How could I know that I was choosing well a second time? I do not think that I could live with a second chance gone wrong. That would just be too horrid a thing."

"But you are older and *wiser* now. You would choose better."

"Would I? I do not know that I would. I *hope* that I would but I fear that I might not."

Gretchen sighed. "You are so much like my brother. Frederick says almost exactly the same sorts of things when I encourage him to get out and give himself a chance to meet a nice young woman."

I thought briefly and then, "Perhaps in his own due time, he will rally and believe again. His trouble is behind him, in a very real sense, and so maybe he can find faith someday soon."

"I hope so. I truly do."

"And he has you and your mother, and your father too, to guide him to a far better match the second time. He will listen to your counsel in future because of his sad past."

"Perhaps yes, perhaps he will. And you know that I would do my utmost to steer him towards a good woman who will love and care for him as she should and as he deserves."

"And so, while you are here visiting, you must do all you can to help raise your brother's faith for a happy future with a new and goodly wife."

"Yes."

I waited for more conversation from Gretchen's side. Beyond my own command, my mind went up the stairs. I had thought the piano silent all this while, but then I finally heard it quietly playing. Perhaps Frederick had been playing all along but I was too lost in my conversation with the always engaging Gretchen to have noticed. I also surmised that Frederick was likely keeping his resting or sleeping mother in mind. I thought that he did not wish to disturb her with any loud pounding of keys. The song was what I would call gentle. Something one could sleep to, I supposed. It was perfect for the moment, certainly.

I liked to think that Frederick was a caring and compassionate son to his mother. And then I thought that I was thinking about Frederick too much. I told myself that perhaps it would be better to go back to calling him the musician in my mind, instead of calling him by his name. Somehow, that seemed too intimate a title for me to bandy about in my brain. I was married after all, though so unhappily, but I could not allow myself to think of Gretchen's brother any more than necessary. I feared to think on him so fondly.

Gretchen breathed in and out at length before speaking again, "And what of you and *your* own happiness?"

"My children: my happiness is in my children, and giving them as happy a life as I can."

"But what of *you*? Would not a happier Isabelle make a happier mother and thus, happier children?"

"Yes, of course, but I have no power there. As for me, I am in the midst of my wilderness in my way, and so true hope in a certain quarter is not possible for me. Those hopes are past into my earlier history."

Gretchen's face seemed so very sad to me.

I thought to lighten the mood and take us both elsewhere, "Though I have shared teatime with your mother before, I have never seen *this* particular set of cups and plates."

She smiled. "Oh, I would imagine not. My mother always has these tucked away. I don't know if she ever uses them. She may never have. They are the best set, you see. Her wedding set, all the way from Germany."

I was shocked, just a little. "Oh my, should we be using them?"

Gretchen laughed in her delightful way, "Of course! I believe in taking every opportunity to spoil myself as a rule, and especially *now* in my condition. I am a princess and a queen all at once. Besides, what good does a beautiful set of cups and plates do sitting in the back of the cabinet or all boxed up in a cupboard or closet? They were created to be enjoyed, I should say, and so I shall enjoy them, even if at my own peril where my mother is concerned when she finds out that I have used them."

I am certain that my face must have shown some severe concern and even shock at the idea of my dear Gretchen being in trouble with her mother for using the tea things, and my part in all of it in the bargain.

"Oh, dearest Isabelle, worry not. My mother will forgive my indulgence with her treasures, for I am growing a better treasure for her, am I not?"

How could I argue such a point? I nodded my head, and smilingly so.

Gretchen laughed pleasingly again, "My mother may mind, but she will not scold me. Her mind is fixed upon my baby more and more these days. She cannot but cherish me for it. And so I take advantage of the situation and my condition. All dainties taste better on better plates, do you not think?"

"Oh yes, of course. Half the pleasure of eating and drinking is the service you use at table."

We each took our last sips and nibbles. And upstairs, Frederick continued quietly playing his gently beautiful music. It was almost as if the soothing sound of falling waters. I tried to keep my soul from soaring, and my mind from thinking of him.

26
To Church

My husband smiled somewhat slyly at me, "And so, my mother tells me that you have been making at least *one* new friend?"

I did not disagree. Indeed, I did not answer.

"Isabelle? Who is this friend? What is her name?"

I simply stated, "Gretchen."

"Is she *pretty*? You know how I *love* to flirt with pretty young ladies."

"Yes, she is very pretty, I should say."

"Then invite her over that she may be *my* friend as well."

"I shan't."

"Then maybe I will go to church to meet her there. Is she a pious little church-going woman like you, Isabelle?"

"I do not think that you should bother her."

"Why not? Ladies *love* to be trifled with."

"She has a husband."

"Well, I will be very good and only go *so* far with my friendly flirting then. It is all in fun, as you well know."

"But I do not think that you should bother to flirt with her, since she loves her husband so very much."

He surprised me with, "And what of you, Isabelle? Do *you* love your own husband so much?"

I bluntly spoke the truth, "Perhaps I did *once* upon a time long ago."

"But not *now*?"

"I think not."

He seemed somewhat amused, "And *why* not?"

"Because you do not deserve it, and you have not been worthy of my love for quite some time... if you *ever* were."

"You are very lucky that I know you are teasing, for I could become very angry if I thought that you were serious."

"I *am* serious."

"Well, well, perhaps I do not care."

"I *know* that you do not care."

"And so, you do not love me."

"It is all of your own making. You could have easily made me love you, and kept me loving you, if only you had treated me rightly."

"Oh, and so what do I make you do, then?"

"You might as well try to make me hate you."

"And so I've made you hate me?"

"I *try* not to hate you, perhaps only for the sake of our children and your mother."

He as much as scoffed, "How very *generous* of you to try not to hate me, Isabelle. Maybe you could force yourself instead to love me for their sakes."

"No, you make *that* impossible."

"What of it? You said I don't care."

"You don't and you *know* it."

He changed the subject to some other thing. I did not care what. I did not bother joining in at all. I turned my focus to my children and left my husband to his mother. Yes, he was returned. He was suddenly back once more, and I was unhappy with *that* miserable situation.

My husband decided to come to church that week. I thought his only reason was to meet Gretchen to try to flirt with her to attempt in his usual type of tormenting me. I easily managed to have our children sit between my husband and me, and with Grandmother Ramstock so delighted that her dear son had come with us, she locked her arm in his, negating any need for me to attempt to feign a want to do so. He sat by her, he walked with her; he visited her friends with her. He played at being delighted to be there. Perhaps he was enjoying himself in his way, for I was certain that he knew I felt discomfort with him simply being there. I knew he was looking for Gretchen. He was hoping to meet her.

Most everyone in the place had noticed *another* young man in attendance for a change. There were whispers and I thought that almost every mind was wondering 'who' was sitting with the Weiss family. They had come in just a little late. *He* was there, you see. Yes, the musician. He had come with his family. Frederick Weiss had come to church that Sunday.

They left a little early. The musician was out in the carriage with his parents before the congregation began to let out of the church. Gretchen did not even delay for chatting as was her usual practice. She too went out to leave as soon as could be accomplished. Only a few words with me, and then she was gone, and swiftly thereafter they were all gone away towards their home.

My husband found his way to me, "Was that your friend Gretchen that I saw you speaking briefly with? You are right. She is a *very* pretty young woman. I am so saddened that I could not meet her. Why did you not introduce me to her?"

I was irritated but complied with a calm answer, "She was in a hurry. There was no time."

"And so, your friend Gretchen has a brother, I understand. You did not tell me that she had a *brother*. He seems a *handsome* fellow. Why did you keep him secret from me? Shall I be jealous of him? Is there something going on with you and he that I should know about? You look very suspicious just now, my dear bride. And so, how well do you know the dashing brother?"

"I have never met him. Today in church was the first time I ever saw him."

"Oh *really*? My mother tells me that you sometimes work for his mother. You work in his house. And yet you profess that you have never even met the fellow? Now, considering the situation, your claim of having never met him is highly suspicious in and of itself. Perhaps I should not go away so soon as I usually am inclined to do. Maybe I need to stay and defend my property from him."

"He has always been upstairs whenever I have been there in the house."

"Yes, I have heard of the rumors. He is some sort of musical madman pounding on his piano upstairs all the day long, and even at night. How *strange* he must be."

I did not answer my husband. I only tried breathing calmly and looked elsewhere, feigning boredom or something akin to it.

He continued, "And so, he mopes upstairs in his set of rooms for some odd reason? How *sad* for you. I am truly sorry for you, Isabelle. I had thought that perhaps you had made a conquest of him. Well, maybe I will defer my jealousy a while longer then. I will give you time to catch him first. And then we will have a row over him, relative to you."

I looked at my husband in true anger, "Oh, don't be so utterly ridiculous."

He laughed aloud. "Oh! I have struck a chord of some sort. I see the flash in your eyes. You have loved him from afar, I think. Unrequited love, I wager. What an amusement for me to know that you are heartsick over this recluse musician."

I only turned away and walked off towards my children.

27
Hiding Coins

Very swiftly after my husband had come back home for his little stay this time, I had decided to swiftly go over to ask Mrs. Weiss if I might take a little time off of working for her because of my husband being returned. She graciously complied. While I was at it, I left a little note for Gretchen, asking her forgiveness for my anticipated general unavailability for the same reason.

Of course I would not be taking on any other work for a while and beyond taking little walks close to home, I planned to mostly stay in or near the Ramstock house. I did not wish to give my husband any miniscule reason to harass me over time away from the house, and thought the situation a good opportunity to take more time for my children, which I usually was inclined towards wanting to do anyway.

One evening, shortly after his return, as he had sometimes done before, he brought up the subject of my money in the following fashion, "I have noticed that you are not out these past days selling yourself as a washer woman or whatever it is that you do for coin of late."

I somewhat evasively answered, "I only work now and then anyway."

"My mother tells me that you are often gone from the house."

"I sometimes take walks nearby, as you know."

"From what I gather, Isabelle, you must have been making enough money that, beyond your meager fashions and whatever else you spend it on, you must have a few coins to spare tucked away somewhere."

I tried not to irritate, "I typically make a few coins, you are quite right, and as you say, though meager, my fashions are what I tend to spend my little money on."

"But Isabelle, I know you well enough to believe that you have some earnings hidden away somewhere."

"You have many times found whatever I have hidden."

"Yes, as I said, you are inclined to save and hide some of your money. Well?"

"Well what?"

"Where have you hidden your savings this time?"

"Why do you think I hide money anymore? Do you think that I would still tuck away money just so that you can find it and spend it? My coin, as we both rightly call it, has generally been hard enough earned. I don't leave my children with your mother, and walk round about to gather work in exchange for a little money, so that you can spend it for me."

He quickly became rather irritable and stern, "Isabelle. Where is your money?"

I told a half truth to guard my savings, "What money? I have learned to spend it as soon as I get it. You have taught me *that* much. As I said, why keep and leave it for you to find and spend?"

He was really beginning to show his growing anger now, "Isabelle, I know that you are disgustingly frugal and apt to save as much as you can. I am sure you have a little money hidden somewhere around here. Tell me where it is or I will *beat* it out of you."

I defied him, "If you hit me even *once*, I will cry out. I will scream so that your mother will hear me."

"Oh, what will she *care*? What will she do? She will do *nothing*. You will only embarrass yourself."

"I don't care if I embarrass myself, for I will embarrass *you* in the process."

"How will *I* be embarrassed if my stupid wife hollers from

being hit by me?"

"I will wear my bruises *publicly* afterwards."

"You wouldn't *dare*. You always cover them."

"I will hide them no longer."

He almost pleaded now, "Isabelle, please give me your money. I need a little to get by. You can earn some more later."

I dared, "You embarrass *yourself* now."

He seemed a little confused. "What do you mean?"

"What husband of *any* stature takes coin from his lowly washer woman wife?"

He was frustrated now. "Isabelle. I need some money. I know that you must have at least a few coins stashed away somewhere around here. Don't make me turn our room upside down."

"Don't bother exerting yourself lifting anything. There is no money in our room."

He paused and then, suspiciously, "Oh, I see. Of course, you no longer hide your money in *our* room. You have hidden money in our children's room, I am certain of it."

"Don't tear into their room either. Don't make a fool of yourself."

He grabbed my arm and squeezed with a twisting motion which hurt a good deal, "Give me your money, Isabelle. *All* of it: I want all that you have saved."

I threatened (though such a threat from me was truly somewhat of an empty one), "Your mother will see that bruise tomorrow. I will make certain of it."

His voice grew louder, "Isabelle. Don't make me truly hurt you."

I readied myself for blows. "Make your *own* coin."

He lost whatever restraint was remaining and threw me into the wall. I was thrown against the plastered wood with some force and then fell hard down onto the floor. I wanted to cry out, but I suppose it is not my way. I was not cognizant of what came out of my mouth. Whatever noises escaped my lips were not likely as loud as the noise of my body bashing into the wall and floor. Indeed, the elder Mrs. Ramstock called up from below, something to the effect of asking if anything was the matter?. I was sure that she thought something large had fallen and perhaps broken. I did not answer. I did not know what to answer. Her son said nothing as well. He was shocked into a calm, in a way. I wanted to tell him to go ask his mother for some money. Heaven knew that she had far more savings than I. 'Why did my husband not ask his father for money?' I wondered. I supposed that it was embarrassing to him to ask either of his parents for money and I sensed that Mr. Ramstock the elder did not appreciate his son asking him for money over and over again. No, the father was not generally proud of the son. I would never say that those two men were close in any way.

My husband exasperatedly left the house, leaving me to come up with an explanation for his mother as to why there was a thumping noise emanating from his room. I simply said not to worry; nothing had broken, and left her with any confusion or conclusion she might wish to imagine.

Yes, I did have some coin hidden. To my own mind, a good deal of money, actually. Over the years, I had become better at hiding my money, and hiding my thoughts from my husband as well. I did not wish to lie to him, but I would not part with the money that I had worked for and had saved for a future day when I might have to leave this man or this house. And thus, he was gone once more.

28
My Parents

I tried to be a good sister to my brothers and sisters. I would cook and clean for them as if I were their mother. I tried to make up the gap for our missing, lax and neglectful parents. I could not limit myself, to myself. In that situation, it seemed incumbent upon at least me to do whatever I could to hold the family together in some form of normalcy. I had to do my part, for to do otherwise was surely negligent or worse.

No, I was not the eldest and I was not either parent in our home, but I knew that the story of my life was before God's eyes, always even as I wrote it in my actions or inactions, and regardless of any sins of omission that any other member in my family might be guilty of, my salvation depended upon my *own* choices. I believed, yes I knew, that I was my brother's keeper, so to speak.

My mother was off and gone, you see, almost as often as my father. She was usually likely at the saloon drinking and embarrassing herself, sometimes with other men. The sordid news travelled round and about long before me or my siblings could possibly be old enough to be cognizant of the gossip that dallied to and fro regarding our mother. As I have eluded already, our father was no saint either, but for some reason, the busy-bodies of our territory tended to forgive our father where they would never forgive our mother. Perhaps it was because the tongue-waggers were mostly women. I have long-since learned that many women do not generally tend to go easy on other women. Many women might overlook the improprieties of some men, but rarely do they let another woman off for any similar dalliance.

I have spoken of my sisters before, and how they seem to have married. I know very little of them and the rest of my family now, for none write to me regularly. Indeed, it is truly rare that I ever read from any one of them. I send letters now and then, but I have learned not to expect any answers to my questions. Even still, as far as I can tell, my brothers, two older and one younger, eventually went off and married women very much like our mother and sisters. I cannot think that *those* women would have improved my brothers' lives or characters at all.

My parents do not come to my mind very often. They have had little positive impact on my life. I confess that I do not like to think of them. I think of my brothers and sisters more often. I feel sadness, to be sure. There is a certain heartbreak; that they cannot be to me what I imagine as anywhere near ideal. We are not the family we could have been. We are not siblings with friendships we could have offered each other. I did *try* to set that kind of example that would have resulted in a togetherness of spirit amongst us, but it eventually became impossible, especially with my sisters. I could not imagine betraying them in the ways that they did to me.

When I *do* think on my parents, it is usually to try to learn from their mistakes. I do not wish to repeat their histories. I want to be like better people. I realize that their mistakes have likely rippled as if water in a pond to affect my own life, and that is why I think about how I might reach far higher than they did. I want to follow better lives. I can follow my mother-in-law to some degree, particularly where the motherly efforts are concerned, but where I cannot find angelic examples to follow, I simply imagine Heavenly ones.

29
Forgetting in the Midst

In recent times of my life reflections, I would sometimes dig out my journal from years past. What I still had in book form was a fraction of what I had originally written. Yes, if you can imagine it, dear reader, I had burned my own little books along the way: most of them, anyway. My daily journals where I honestly expressed my feelings relating to current life in those times did sometimes reveal a deal of injury.

As a youth, when I painfully poured out my heart into my little books of life, I would sometimes say too much: far too much. Thus, in the midst of fears of being discovered and getting beaten for it, I would burn what I had written. I knew the realities of crossing my father or mother. I had many times suffered the bruises to prove it. They simply would not be criticized in any shape or form, particularly by their children. I knew that neither of my parents would be opposed to looking for and finding my diary, and then enact a punishment for anything I would have said against them.

My life with my husband had been no different in this way. I had scribbled my tears into books, and then I had destroyed them. I could not get caught. I feared what my husband would do to me if he knew what I fully thought of him. Nevertheless, some of my writings for myself had survived throughout it all. I had a little while back found something I had written, what seemed an eternity ago...

"It is the eve of my wedding. I am to be married tomorrow. I believe it a wonderful new beginning for me: a fresh start. I feel blissful: entirely and thoroughly happy, as if floating up into the air and flying throughout the clouds. I cannot sleep. I do not care regarding my hair or my dress. That was all planned out weeks ago when I cared so very much about that sort of thing. But now, now all I can think of is that I will be *his* wife tomorrow. And we will be off on our wedding journey. I will say farewell to the young girl that I was before I became engaged to my handsome and charming Mr. Ramstock. I say adieu to my Barrett family. I will no longer belong to them as I have heretofore done. Now I will belong to my husband."

I could not help but cry at this discovery. When had I last read it? I know that I had not *wished* to read such naiveté from me for a very long time. It is too painful a thing to recall. I was so very full of hope. I held onto so much faith back then. I believed. I trusted that I had found freedom from want and suffering. I thought that I was taking a step into perfect happiness, but little did I yet know that I was stepping onto the precipice of pain, and then I fell into a hellish abyss as a young married woman.

And now, I try to live my half life, attempting to forget that I am married to a beast. If I think on my children, I can find joy. My children are my world. They are my Heaven on earth. Through all the unhappiness, I am grateful for joyfulness in my children, and I can be thankful that my horrid husband is near always gone from me.

Beyond my children, there is no banquet table before me. No, I have found my way to being happy with crumbs, even from off the ground. When need be, I cope with my emptiness by plucking up what fallen crumbs I can. Until lately, I had been taking pleasures in the sounds of the musician's piano playing. Even his lamenting violin had brought some kind of edification to me from time to time. I was fed by that music. Were these guilty pleasures? Certainly not before I knew that he was a young man, and eligible for marriage (though he is not currently in that frame of mind). Once I knew a little of Frederick Weiss, I did my utmost to think *not* of him. Leaving his music to the ears and souls of others has been most difficult for me. This has meant a type of starvation. My relatively recent lifeline has been cut to a great degree. Attempting to be good in this way has left me in the darkness.

The music that lives in the upper floor of the Weiss house was lifeblood to me many months past. I believed in something again. Once more I felt that I was a living being. Though once I knew that I dare not think much of the musician; oh but what herculean measures my mind had to go through in order to sit in the Weiss house and not think of Frederick as he played. How could I not? It was almost impossible. I forced myself to make a division between the music and the man. I told myself that I could admire the music but I could not esteem and wonder about the man who played it. I should not know much of him, but only his music. I supposed that I could think of the musician without thinking much on Frederick.

The music had helped me forget my misery in marriage. That one especial song had given me a place in time to live once more. I felt as if a woman again: not only a mother, but as a woman once more. The individual that I had once been (or tried to be and had hoped to become), had been stolen away from me by my cruel husband, in a very real and true sense. Yes, what my parents had not managed to destroy in me, my husband had picked up and carried on from, in demeaning my spirit almost to a type of death. I wished to forget the man who had owned me as husband, sometimes in body, but never really in soul.

As needs must, I have also attempted to continually forget the man who is the musician.

30
The Musician

As quickly as my husband had gone away again, I had gone to see Gretchen. I did not allow myself to look forward to hearing Frederick's music, however. His sister's friendship was in its way a fulfilling substitute for what his music had come to mean to me prior to her coming. As an unhappily married young woman, I knew that I must put up a barrier between myself and my love for Frederick's songs and his magnificent playing of them. I could not allow myself to cross over a line from admiring musical genius to finding attraction in the man who played that inspiring music.

Thank Heavens for Gretchen, I thought. I loved her. As a sister and a dear friend to me, I had come to love and feel eternally grateful for her. Through her, I could enjoy her brother's music while still standing afar off from him in a sense, but beyond that disconnected connection, in and of herself, Gretchen was a wonder to me. With or without her musician brother, I would have counted my blessings in becoming her friend.

Gretchen and I were barely sat down to chat in the Weiss parlor with a tea tray between us; when Frederick appeared at the doorway. I gasped: audibly. I attempted to compose myself. All my thoughts about avoiding thinking of him, and then, there he was standing before me. I looked away. My resolve in choosing rightly near dissolved. Instantly, I struggled with my desire to know him, if only as a friend and as if my brother too. I knew that I should not. He was dangerous territory to me: beautiful territory. I could *not* dare to move towards him, even in my mind. His music had been and meant so very much to me, and I knew that I must hold firm to a great separation between us.

I saw at once that he was there at the parlor entrance to ask Gretchen something. His eyes had turned my way just briefly. Our gazes had connected only momentarily.

All he said was, "Gretchen?"

And she was promptly up and into the entryway and then beyond to talk to him. I had not noticed if she had asked to be excused by me or not. My mind was filled with the musician, even as I tried desperately not to think of him in any way. In that instant, the image of his visage was impressed upon my mind in a way that I could not shake it away. I could think nor feel of nothing else for the moment. No, I did not think of his handsome face. It was something else entirely.

On his face I saw the pain that was my life. I saw into and behind his eyes, a sorrow that seemed something like I had known far too long. I thought all at once that we were kindred spirits. I felt that we were kindred in our regrets, with a spiritual connection of related betrayals. It was as if I knew him instantly. It felt as if I had known him forever. Yes, I had surely known a good deal of his music, and I had felt *that* connection to him for such a length of time, but this was unexpectedly more.

And though I had wholly felt deep in despairing pity for myself many a time; seeing his worn and almost scarred spirit written outwardly to me, caused my own self-pity to dissolve away to near nothing in the face of his obvious tragedy. How could I think of myself when his pained face was before my mind's eye, his heart seeming broken beyond repair? I thought that surely he had suffered similarly or perhaps more than I. If that were *not* so, even if my sufferings were greater, deeper and more protracted than his, I could not focus on my own pains long-since, for my heart could only seem to feel for him above and beyond myself. I could think on my own lost life as almost naught when I was staring into the losses that I felt he must have undergone.

THE MUSICIAN

The sensations I was processing relative to the musician, and my reactions to his sorrows versus my own, reminded me of my motherly instincts relative to my children and whenever their pains of accident or sadness would quickly wash away any depression I might be feeling in those moments. At any given time, even if during those times when I felt lost down into the depths of despairing, a little cry or even the least trifle of a need from one of my children, and I would be shocked back into the reality of being a mother. The little child of woe that I could have been feeling in and of myself, would fade away in an instant, and my mind and heart would rally for the want or feelings of my child. To possibly be more concise, what I mean to express is that the nurturing mother in me always outweighed the injured child in me.

Yes, I was feeling quite motherly towards the musician. This seemed quite strange to me. He looked to be around my age I thought. Neither Mrs. Weiss nor Gretchen had actually ever told me his age, to my recollection. I had never asked. Frederick could not have been more than a few years younger or older than me, and yet my heart was full of compassion for him in his situation. Yes, I supposed that his lot might seem easier to me at first glance and in certain respects, but on the other hand, I felt great pity for him.

No, he was not suffering any current abuse from his past wife, wherever she may be in the world at this moment in time. His heart had apparently gotten over her marital cruelties sometime before or after his divorce from her was granted. I did not think that he pined for her in any way now. No, he did not need worry over any children of his own. And perhaps his prison was of his own making. He chose not to seek to marry again as yet. Still, he was isolated in his part of his parents' house with only instruments like his piano and violin to keep him company.

As for me, I had and could hold my beloved children to soothe the pains that I felt in the great void of my heart. I was imprisoned by my life partner, but he was gone a good deal. I was free of him oftentimes; and his mother was no true challenge to me. She was kind enough. I was somewhat satisfied in life most times, if I could forget my generally gone husband. I was blessed with some joys, quite actually many joys, particularly in my children.

Yes, Frederick's music was his own solace. And his musical compositions were his creations, almost like his children. Indeed, beyond my children, Frederick's music had been my own solace as well. I could certainly understand his being lost in his music, for I too had been lost enough times in his songs and his playing.

But, as soothing as music could be, even as a prayer of the heart so to speak, when I came to fully think on it, such a comfort paled in comparison to the love for and from one's own children. They were living breathing beings, you see. They were as if angels sent to me from Heaven. They gave love and embraces to me, but more than that, they were my prime reasons for living. And I could not compare the love for one's children to the love of one's music. Yes, poor Frederick knew more sorrow than I. His soul must have ached in a way that I did not know. I loved and was loved by my children.

Yes, I did suppose that to compose a song was something like having children of one's own. Creating music was a type of creating life. Bringing a song to life for the world had its comparison to bringing a child into the world. But it was no true comparison, I felt. A new piece of music, however wonderful, might be an added light to the world, but it was not an angelic life like that of a living, breathing heaven-sent human being. And so I had sat musing.

Gretchen returned to me for our little visit in her family's parlor. She said little of her brother. He had needed to speak to her of something, and she was uncharacteristically guarded with that information. I thought it best that I heard nothing of what Frederick had said to her anyhow. I did not wish to think of him.

I held my children close as they fell asleep that night. I held them a good while longer. I did not wish to leave them. As I had done many times before, I gazed upon their angelic faces in the shining of the single candle flame. My heart was full. I ached to give my dear children everything. I loved them so very dearly. I thanked God with all my soul in an audible whisper for giving me these precious darling souls to guard and nurture in this life's journey. And I prayed that the musician would find more meaningful happiness in his life as well.

31
Beaten Again

I could not believe that he had returned so very soon. Ordinarily, he was gone months. This time, only weeks it seemed. Why was my husband back again? Was he only after my money once more? Could he possibly find my every hiding place? Should I sacrifice some of my savings in one place in the hopes that he would not think to hunt for more? Could he force me into divulging any or all of my funds? Would his beatings be severe enough to get any coin out of me? Or would he instead simply ask his mother, or finally ask his father for more money?

Why did he not discipline himself enough to work for his own money? No, I knew him. He felt entitled to the coins earned by the sweat of the brows of others. He always wanted the quick and easy money. He did not truly believe in working for it; and he was inclined to think that gambling was the way to get money quickly, and how to get more of it. Somehow, he would always seem to forget all his losses and only recall his few wins. Because of the realistic odds, I could never believe in gambling, but he doggedly did.

As was his usual habit, when my husband was returned back home for a time, he always tried to control me as his wife. As had become my usual defense of self, I would not have him as my own husband. I did not respect, honor, obey or even listen to him anymore. I barely acknowledged him. I did not share his room. I would not share his bed. I did not love him and had not done for so very long that I couldn't recall what it was like ever to once have loved him. How could I love him? How can a woman love a husband who treats her ill at every turn, and takes to the beds of who knows what and how many women whenever he is away from his own house and wife?

In some former times, I thought that I should try to fight towards being more of a wife to my husband. But he was no husband to me. I sometimes wondered if I could possibly find the strength and a way to bring our marriage back into being. I used to wonder if I might be able to make a marriage with this man. Could the power be within me to change what was wrong between us for the better? Could I change him? I could possibly change myself in some or perhaps even many ways, but how could I change him? I knew that I had already tried everything I could think of in years past, but I could think of nothing new to try. And I had no heart to do it. I had no strength left in that realm.

I could no longer work at reviving a dead marriage, and I believed more and more that I should not attempt it. Marriage was a sanctified heavenly ordinance and my husband had destroyed that which should have been sacred between us. Was it possibly even blasphemous in a way to pretend at being wife to a husband who was so terribly unworthy of any true wife? I could not do it. No, I had tried, I had attempted to try and I could no longer do it.

No, I could not play wife to a man who was no husband to me. It was quite simply all the women, you see. I could have taken almost anything else. I would have almost happily traded more beatings for a faithful husband. His temper I could forgive. His actions far beyond flirtations I could not forgive. I knew that I should not have to contemplate such injustices, but I did not care about bruises on my body like I did the betrayals of the heart. Much could be forgiven and perhaps forgotten day to day, but some things were not possible. Infidelity was insurmountable to me.

Particularly in more recent times, I would usually not attempt to confront my husband about what he did while he was gone from me, but every now and then I had somehow felt and behaved like an actual wife. I once was inclined to frequently ask him about his life with other women. In those times, there was no better way to provoke his hand or fist against me than to accuse him of betraying our marriage vows.

At the first blows, I was given to tears. I cried a great deal; but the more I wept, the more he beat me. He could not abide my crying. Out of necessity, I learned to choke back my tears. I held my weeping inside myself. Gradually, I learned to turn my tears to hate, I suppose. I did not need cry so much when I harbored hate against my husband instead. My anger was a sufficient emotion. I needed not turn to tears when I was angry. With every hit against me, I focused the pain into hate. His every blow was channeled into my anger.

And then, over time, the anger and hatred settled down into an apathetic attitude. I changed my way with him. I stopped being his wife in my heart, and then my body quickly followed. I simply was forced into that existence by virtue of my spirit. I could not also betray myself, in the ways that my husband continually betrayed me. I could not be his wife, because he was not my husband. In time, I did not care where he went when he left me. I did not care what women he saw and what he might choose to do with them. I only wished that he would not return to bother me. I liked him gone. Then I could live again, at least to some measurable degree.

Early in that first day after my husband's current return, Gretchen had come to call upon me. She thought it was to be one of our usual pleasant little visits. Before I could think of how to warn her of unpleasant possibilities due to my husband being there again in the Ramstock house, he was standing there before us both. Quite a proud peacock he looked, too. I knew what he was about. He felt he had seized upon a sudden triumph over me. He could not seem happier to suddenly see my friend in the house.

Quite charmingly, my husband began, "My dear Isabelle, and so this is your lovely friend Gretchen, I presume?"

I did not smile, though what could I say but, "Yes."

Gretchen smiled slightly and nodded generally towards him.

She looked back to me, as if to say without words that she did not wish to get to know my husband further, and perhaps in the hopes that he would simply leave us ladies be and to our own chatter, without him. He would not be discouraged so easily. He started up with some silly sort of small-talk that would work very well in a saloon, I supposed.

What I saw in my husband as he tried to flirt with my friend seemed quite pathetic to me. Either he had lost his charming touch or I could see so very through it all that it simply sickened me. I felt no jealousy. I felt pity for my friend that she must be subjected to my husband. I also felt such revulsion for this man that I was so sadly married to. I thought him insipidly stupid at least, and more like disgustingly overt. I was thoroughly embarrassed to be called his 'Mrs. Ramstock'.

Gretchen seemed to keep looking at me for a sense of what she should say. I could not help her. I suppose I only looked sad and ashamed for the situation we two were put into because of my libertine husband. At first Gretchen was polite enough in any of her little responses, but then I do think that her patience quickly waned and even perhaps her anger was kindled a little.

My husband continued his attempted advances, so to speak, and looking to me while commenting on Gretchen, buoyantly accused, "My dear wife, I suppose you have kept your beautiful friend from meeting me out of guarded jealousy? You fear I will prefer her over you?"

Oh, my gracious, but I did not know what on earth to say while I blushed with complete embarrassment.

Gretchen did not fear finally storming in with, "Mr. Ramstock, you disgust me twofold with your unguarded flirtations: first, because your beautiful wife deserves a descent husband, of which you obviously are not, and second, because my beloved husband would have at least harsh words for you if he were here to witness your impropriety towards me. Cease and desist, sir, and be gone from us."

My husband's mouth fell agape and held that shocked position for a lengthy moment. Gretchen turned to me, turning her back on my husband. One of her hands reached out to be placed on one of mine. She smiled comfortingly towards me. We seemed to stare at each other, both waiting for my husband to simply leave us. He said nothing in response, finally turned about the other way, and left the parlor. Ashamed or not, I did not know nor care what he felt.

Later, after Gretchen had left the house, my husband took opportunity to find me alone. He said very little but only seemed to hang about, waiting for me to speak. I sensed that he expected me to confront him regarding his abysmal behavior towards my friend and myself. He wanted me to start a quarrel with him about Gretchen. I knew that he did. But what would be the point to that? I thought that Gretchen had done wonderfully at spurning him and putting him in his place. There was no need for me to add salt to his silly wounds. I decided that I should not dignify his bad behavior with any acknowledgements from me. He seemed a stupid spoiled child at not getting what he wanted.

I was contemplating the best instant and opportunity to simply walk away, when my husband abruptly accused, "I see what you are about. It is the *brother*. You are friends with Gretchen because of her brother. Admit it. You are dallying with her brother Frederick."

I fired back in return, "Oh, don't be so tirelessly ridiculous. You are only trying to make me out to be like you. You cannot bring me down to your level as much as you might try. I assure you, I am nothing like you. You have made a mockery of our marriage vows, but I know that my vows are not only with you, but with God. While I could surely be tempted to break my vows with *you* in some way, because you have broken that contract between us long ago, I will *not* break my vow with God. No man, no matter how attractive to me, could cause me to turn my back on God and any promise I have made to *Him* under Heaven."

"I *knew* it! You are besotted by Gretchen's brother. You are *after* him."

"I am after *no* man."

"You pretend to be a friend to Gretchen so you can catch her

165

brother."

"I am a *true* friend to Gretchen. And if I were inclined to try to catch any man, what could I possibly do with him once I caught him? I am a married woman. I am a mother, for Heaven's sake. I am not free to marry and love again. I might as well be a *nun.* As long as you live and I remain married to you, I am not free to consider any other man. Why won't you understand me? I am no harlot. I am not the sinful libertine that *you* are."

His quick and strong slap stung my face severely.

Not dissuaded in the least, I turned further on him, "I *hate* you. I once loved you but you did not deserve my innocent love. You taught me to despise you by all your ill actions and so I hate instead of love you. Other men are of no account to me, for I am true to my vows and what good Christian society expects of me. I would rather live my life alone, in marital loneliness, than submit to being anything like a wife to you. Our marriage has long been over. Go back to your *saloon* girls and leave me to myself."

He slapped me again. Anger or something akin to it strengthened me. Essentially feeling no pain, I willfully looked into his eyes with almost a challenge daring him to hit me again. He obliged. This horrid little pattern continued briefly until I felt more bruised than I had bargained for. For once, I dared to physically strike back with one blow of my own against him. I know not where my little fist even connected upon his larger frame, but my hand hurt, likely more than wherever it was that I had managed to hit him. This defiance and self-defense from me truly angered him. He tore into me with a fury.

For the first time in our marriage, I was entirely afraid of him and what he might end up doing to me. Of course I knew that he had the power to easily kill me. I fully knew that his rage could quickly take him that far. I did not cry out. I don't think I had enough sense for that. I only tried to survive his thrashing. Actually, I think instinctively, I soon played dead. I had long ago done it in childhood. As if now a rag doll, I went limp. His anger gradually diffused. He was done. He left me to myself. I felt an inner prayerful thankfulness to the Heavens above that he was finished, this time.

Usually, when my husband lost his temper and beat me, he was clever enough to hit me where my clothes would generally hide the bruises or marks; but during this offensive event, as sometimes, he couldn't resist going further. He had choked my neck severely and hit my face hard enough to badly bruise one of my cheekbones. When I went to my looking glass afterwards, there were distinct marks on my neck, and my one cheek and eye near it were already beginning their swelling.

My husband would have expected me to stay to my room rather than to let my bruises be seen by even his parents, for this would have been my usual pattern and practice after such an unpleasant event. But I was *not* my usual self. I felt a type of true rebellious vigor. I would not wear my bruises *proudly*, as I had some time ago forewarned him in a type of promise, but I actively decided not to hide them. And so, that night, I went to the dinner table with the red and swelling signs of my husband's mistreatment clearly showing on my neck and face. I saw that my parents-in-law noticed. They looked back and forth at each other a good deal. My husband seemed embarrassed, or something of that nature. He was likely quite angry with me for my insolence.

On the following day, which happened to be a Sunday, I looked far worse. Bruises tend to do that: they look much worse on the second day than the first. And though the bruises on my neck might have been missed by most (because of my higher collar), with the large still-swollen bruise on my face and a blackened eye unmistakable, I went to Church nonetheless. I knew that my husband entirely expected me to stay home with my wounds hidden from view rather than to show them out in public, but I had long since tired of hiding my husband's sins. I told myself that I did not deserve my face being beaten, and so why should I always feel the shame of the marks made on it by my husband? Why was *I* always ashamed, when it was *he* who should have been ashamed of himself? No, in my way I now wanted others to see some of his sins.

I supposed that my parents-in-law managed to overlook my coming to their dinner table with beginning bruises due my husband's battering, but my going to church looking all the worse for the horrid wear (or beatings, to be more precise) was just simply too much. They could less easily ignore my *public* display of their son's husbandry. I do think that my parents-in-law were terribly embarrassed because of the visible situation. At the time, I did strongly suspect that they were angrier at me for showing their world my bruises in the second place, than at their son for pummeling blows upon me in the first place.

The Ramstock men did not come to church, and I dare say that the elder Mrs. Ramstock was thoroughly rethinking whether she should go either, considering my appearance. I instantly saw the painful embarrassment she would be feeling throughout the service, as well as before and afterwards. I did feel badly that she would surely feel so terribly uncomfortable, but I held my ground and stayed determined to go nonetheless. As I think I have suggested before, the elder Mr. Ramstock never tended towards attending the Sabbath service anyway, but the son was obviously planning to go (and without me) until he saw that I was determined to show my battered face to the congregation. That was when my unworthy husband took himself back to his room; and thus it was me, my children, and their grandmother who went. This was highly usual, yes, but my damaged face was not, of course.

Shortly after we returned from church, there was a tremendous argument in the Ramstock house and amongst that small Ramstock clan of three. I had taken my children to their room to dress them out of their church attire and back into their play clothes, and then the yelling had begun, a little in the distance in the house. I heard a little of my mother-in-law's apparent pleadings, my husband's obvious attempts at defending himself, and then it was mostly my father-in-law and his angry chastising. I did not know one word for certain that was said. I could really only imagine. Of course, I could *guess* the overwhelming substance of it. I hid in my children's room with them. I tried to distract them with their toys. I tried not to show my concern for what might happen next. I confess, I feared for our future together.

When all was finally quiet in the Ramstock house, I dared to come out of my children's room, for they were getting terribly hungry. I snuck myself to the kitchen to retrieve a little sustenance for my children and myself, and then swiftly retreated back to their room. Beyond leaving for any necessity, I kept my children in their room with me throughout the rest of that day, evening and that entire night. By morning, all things were still very quiet. By that next day, my husband was obviously gone again, and my father-in-law was very much gone as well. Grandmother Ramstock seemed to be keeping almost entirely to her own room as well, because I saw none of her at least that next day and night.

Well, there had obviously been quite the warring kerfuffle between my husband and his parents. I assumed that I would likely never know even the half of what had transpired. I knew that neither my husband nor his father would ever breathe a word of it to me, and I could handily imagine that my mother-in-law would likely as not be telling me anything. That was her way. The entire thing would turn into a non-subject. Of course I knew that I was a large part and parcel of the argument: at least the fact that my husband had bruised me and that I had shown my bruises to the world of the town around them. For shame, I easily supposed. How could he let his wife go *out* like that? What would everyone *think* of them?

I wondered if my husband had been scolded by his father for not controlling his temper, or for not controlling his wife better, or perhaps for both. I suspected that the three Ramstocks would not have expected me to take my bruises to church. I saw the shock in their faces when I was up and ready to go. But what could they say in that moment, with the few servants in attendance around us? I said nothing, as if nothing was amiss or at least unusual, and so we women and children went to church as usual. I had thought that the Ramstock father and son might argue some whilst the rest of us attended church, and for all I know, they did a deal of that. I doubt Ramstock the elder allowed his son to hide in his room the entire time.

You can imagine that I would not like to be thrown out into the street for my impudence and effrontery to the Ramstock family, dear reader, but beyond that practical sort of thing, I did not truly care if the elder Mr. and Mrs. Ramstock were angry at me for publicly showing the bruises that their son had so generously given: bestowed in blows upon me. Perhaps they should have taught him far better long before, or at least counseled him a little better more recently. In any event, all that type of related unpleasantness would most likely pass (if not completely and quickly), with both Ramstock men gone afar off and I hoped it all would be eventually forgotten. I did not believe that the Ramstock family wished to remember that sort of sordid detail in their own history. People tend to like to move on from their own faults, and to forget their follies.

32
A Divorcement?

After the fact, I briefly wondered if I should not have taken my bruises out into public. For quite some time I felt very badly for Grandmother Ramstock. I cannot say that even for a moment I felt badly for my husband or maybe even his father, but I did regret that I had caused embarrassment to my mother-in-law. She was a good and kind woman, after all. No, she was not a perfect being, and she was not all to me that I needed in a woman as my friend, but she was wonderful to my children and always treated me kindly as well.

I trusted and hoped that any of the embarrassment to my mother-in-law would gradually fade into a distant memory of past regrets. Perhaps more my regrets than hers, but I did believe that each of us would tend to forget the unpleasant episode that had just transpired amongst the Ramstocks. The men were gone from the house, which aided in our forgetting the incident. Neither my mother Ramstock nor I spoke to each other about any of it.

My mother-in-law was keeping to herself at home more than usual and I felt assured that she would not appreciate any company coming over to her house, so to preempt or prevent Gretchen from coming to call, I decided to go and call upon my friend at her parents' house before she could attempt the same at mine. Grandmother Ramstock easily agreed to tend my children while I went out for a long walk. I did not tell her that I was going to the Weiss home, simply in case that knowledge might cause her any discomfort or distress. I did not know what my husband might have said to his mother about his possible suspicion or frivolous accusation about me having designs upon the Weiss son.

I had not been working in the Weiss home for a while, and I could not currently use work as any excuse for going there. As much as Gretchen had become my dear friend, if my husband wanted his mother convinced that my friendship with Gretchen was only my ruse to get closer to her brother, then I did not want to fan that false flame in any way. No, it was better for me not to tell all to my mother Ramstock, at least in this case.

Gretchen welcomed me in most graciously. Compassion was written all across her face. She had not seen me excepting only from afar since that last day at church, and had not talked to me up close at all since that day before. Now finally seeing me in person thusly, she promptly embraced me and held me in a motherly fashion at a little length.

After letting go of me, she pulled back and looked into my eyes while tenderly asking, "Are you all right, my poor Isabelle? I have been so worried about you."

"Yes, yes, do not worry about me, Gretchen. It was nothing."

"*Nothing*? Your face did not *look* like nothing. I could barely keep from crying for you right there in the church, and I have wept for you since."

I dare say I must have sounded a little recklessly flippant when I replied with, "Well, I have been beaten by him before. I always survive it."

Gretchen was all concern for me, "But, how can you *live* like that, Isabelle? How can you bear it?"

"Because I must."

"How often does he beat you?"

"Well, if I behave myself and am a very *good* wife, I can keep him from hitting me. You see, I brought it on myself. I provoked him a little."

"Provoked him? How?"

"Oh, it is of no consequence now. I was defiant, and I knew I would get hit hard for my attitude. I should have bit my tongue, and then I could have saved my face the bruising."

"But…" She seemed a little out of words: a little incredulous. She wasn't quite sure what to say or ask.

I took the opportunity to thank her, "Oh, Gretchen, I wanted to thank you for giving my husband your cold shoulder for my sake, good woman that you are. Yes, all women should be like you. Thank you for not flirting back with my husband, and not humiliating me like he wanted to do with you."

She looked a little shocked. "But, what else would I *do* under the circumstance? On three counts I could not have capitulated to his unsubtle nuances. My *husband* would not like me to flirt in return, *you* would not deserve such treatment from your friend in *any* case, and I am not inclined to like that sort of dalliance anyway. I save all my flirtatiousness for my own husband."

"Exactly. Rightly so. I think as you do, Gretchen. Nevertheless, thank you again and again."

"No thanks are needed, Isabelle. What good woman on earth would take part in that sort of sport?"

"Well, I fear that too many women *do*."

"No. Not *good* women, at least. And for my part, I simply cannot think that *ill* of women in general."

"I'm sorry to say *yes*, it is too true. I have seen it too often. My *sisters*, for example."

"Oh, *no*! Your *sisters*? Not your own sisters! They have joined in with your husband in flirtations against you?"

"Yes, well, that is the kind of women they grew into."

"How could that *be*? How could sisters of *yours* be those kinds of women?"

"Well, I am sorry to say it, but they tend to take after our mother."

Gretchen was suddenly silent. Again, she did not know what to say in return.

I continued with a little explanation that actually explained very little, "But that is another story that I would rather not tell for now. Suffice it for me to say that I try not to be anything like my mother."

Gretchen's eyes were quite wide as her tongue was very silent. I thought that she had never imagined that *my* own mother was not as good a woman as my husband's mother. I suspected she had never thought that my mother was a woman not to be followed. She had simply assumed that my mother was at least as good as her own, in any case. Why would she have thought otherwise?

Without much contemplation, I blurted in another direction, or sort of back to the beginning, "I've decided to better behave myself, however. Even though I have always managed to mend after one of my husband's beatings, his temper can be riled beyond his ability to control it, and I might suffer far more than I bargain for one day. Maybe in and of myself I would not care so much if my husband killed me sometime, but I must not provoke him to anger, at least for the sake of my children. I must live for them."

Gretchen looked profoundly sad as well as full of compassion, "Oh, Isabelle. You must live for yourself too. Yes, your children need you, but you must think more well of yourself and your life. If nothing else, would it not be a sort of blasphemy to despair so, and to hold your life so cheaply?"

I was fully repentant for my irresponsible comment, "Yes, you are right."

She leaned in close to sincerely ask, "But, cannot you get a divorcement from your husband, like Frederick did with his horrid wife?"

"I am certain that it must not be possible. I wish that it was, but my husband will never formally admit to his infidelities with other women, all which I cannot prove anyhow, and I am certain that my occasional bruises are of no consequence under the laws of the land. I cannot afford to take him on in court in any case."

Gretchen truly wanted to offer me a helping hand, "But, perhaps there is a way. Maybe my father could consult with someone who might know if there is a way for you. Then someday, you could marry again."

I smiled. "Sometimes I think or dream of or hope for such

a possibility, but then again, where would my children and I go until then? How would we eat? How could I possibly afford to care well for my children? If there was a way for me to divorce my husband, how could I possibly stay in his mother's house like I do? How would my children fully benefit from her care, like they do? I have been saving money in case I am forced out on my own by my husband in some way, someday; but I do not hope for that kind of poverty and danger for my children. No, I had my chance at marriage and I lost in the bargain. I have long accepted that. My thoughts are not for me, but for my children and *their* future. I am happy to sacrifice my own dreams for the good of my children."

She leaned in close again and whispered, "Isabelle, you are so much like my brother. I know he does not have children to worry about, but, like you, Frederick thinks that he had only one given chance at marriage and he blames himself far more for the failure of it than he should. Indeed, I should say that he carries no blame at all. Everything lies at the feet of that horrid woman."

"From what you have told me, Gretchen, I should certainly say that your brother owns no blame whatsoever. You should convince him to rally and try again. Surely he could find the hope and faith to believe that he could finally be happy in marriage? He deserves no less."

"Oh yes, he is very deserving on that count. Like you, he deserved to be happy in marriage but was cheated out of what was due him. When I think of you and Frederick and your sad stories, I am all the more grateful to have been so lucky in love. I have been very fortunate in the choice of my husband."

"Gretchen, you give me at least hope that not all the world is miserable in marriage. At least I can believe in marriage from afar because of happy wives like you."

Genuine caring was written on her face as she said, "Oh, Isabelle! I wish that you could get out of that marriage and find the right man for you. I wish you equal felicity in life."

"I have my children. That is enough."

I knew by the look on her lovely face that Gretchen was

still thoughtfully pondering the possibilities of helping me to obtain a bill of divorcement from my husband, even as I sat there knowing how impossible such a thing would be for me to try for or accomplish, and then to live with the aftermath and consequences of it. For the sakes of my two children, I could not do it. I could not even consider it.

33
On First True Acquaintance

In mutual anticipation of their upcoming angelic arrival, Gretchen's husband had finally come. Upon this knowledge, I had purposely stayed away. I did not wish to intrude at all. I thought that Gretchen would want her husband to herself a good while. I did not think that she should need me visiting while she had her husband there with her. I did not think I need meet him beyond the nods and smiles at church, but it wasn't too very long before I received an invitation to the Weiss house for an evening's visit.

Yes, Gretchen wished me there to dinner. My children were invited to come as well. It was just like Gretchen to include my children and to invite us each and all to a fine evening meal. I thought better of the idea though, at least the entire idea. In the end, I chose to leave my children with their grandmother, to be tucked in to their beds at their usual fairly early bedtime, while I went to the Weiss home on my own for a late dinner.

As to any possible suspicions on the elder Mrs. Ramstock's side regarding my feelings or intentions towards the young Mr. Weiss or any implications in my seeing this said musician, I simply chose not to face that thought. I would wait and see if I could see anything in the way of concerns written on my mother-in-law's face. I could not. All seemed well on that front.

My mother Ramstock was all kindness and generosity as was her usual self. 'Of course she would tend to the children while I enjoyed a night's dinner out in company', and I was given a horse and buggy for the purpose as well. My mother-in-law did not think it wise for me to go out for a lengthy night's entertainment and more precisely, to walk both ways in the dark. I would have done it anyhow, for I was full of courage in such things if I was thoroughly determined to accomplish something, but I did truly appreciate the safety, ease and comfort of accommodation in driving rather than walking such a two ways distance late at night.

Once arrived into the Weiss home, the delightful spirit of the evening seemed set when, in that instant, I saw the perfectly amiable Mr. Douglas Jennings standing there with his arm around his lovely glowing (and growing) wife. I had already been cordially and thoroughly introduced to Gretchen's husband, before we were all begun in the happy prospect and process of sitting down to table. Frederick was not in the room as yet. I could not help but look for him. I tried not to. Indeed, I was determined not to think of him. I feared myself thinking of him. It was not that I could not thoroughly control myself in such a circumstance, but simply that I knew that I was certainly a human being and not beyond at least little temptations if I did not put up barriers for myself against that which was taboo. I did not fear adhering to the letter of the law, but I wished to hold fast and firming to the spirit of the moral law as well. Even what only I knew could hurt me eternally.

I supposed that some might have suspected that Frederick could be the sort of person who liked to cause suspense regarding himself, and thereby came late to the event; but because of all that I already knew about him, I believed that his nervous shyness and reserved nature kept him from all of us until that last minute that it was absolutely necessary for him to enter the room. I doubted he enjoyed the idea of an evening's dinner and entertainment with me added to the family table. I thought that he must be more comfortable with just his family, but I was not a part of that family. I was as if an intruding guest.

Frederick was suddenly simply there. He had quietly entered the room and taken his place at the table. All the hubbub and chatter had given him cover. Perhaps he had cautiously waited for that type of distraction to allow him opportunity to sneak in, so to speak. As you might see, dear reader, I thought on these little nuances of things, especially as regarding the musician. Yes, I did think of him, at least somewhat.

Gretchen began, "Oh, Frederick! You are finally come! Well, I must, at long last, properly introduce you to my very best friend in all and around the town, if not the world. Frederick, please meet my dearest Isabelle."

He nodded my way. I thought I detected the tiniest fraction of a smile.

I returned a much more obvious smile, my own little nod towards him and, "It is so nice to finally meet you, Mr. Weiss."

Gretchen put in, "Oh *please*, Isabelle! Call him Frederick. You are surely like my sister, and so, please be as a sister to my brother?"

I smilingly obliged, "I'm very pleased to meet you, Frederick."

Gretchen then turned to her brother, "Now, Frederick. It is *your* turn. Please greet my friend by her name."

Frederick seemed highly uncomfortable but he obeyed nonetheless, "And I am pleased to meet you as well, Isabelle."

I thought that Frederick's discomfort permeated the room and a slight unease persisted momentarily. If I did not think I knew better, I might have thought that Gretchen could not help herself from almost playing as matchmaker between Frederick and myself. This was highly inappropriate, of course, but Gretchen was like a free spirited and wild horse that could never be entirely tamed by conventions. I instantly forgave her the possible indiscretion as I was fairly certain everyone else in the room would, if they had noticed anything at all amiss anyhow. I chose to let my suspicion or her inadvertent hint be forgotten almost even as it had happened. Ignoring what might have been intended seemed the thing to do.

The lovely meal progressed as the numerous courses were served, one after another. Everything was beautifully delicious and the conversation was pleasant. Frederick said very little and I confess that I was not terribly chatty either. I felt somewhat reserved and even shy, preferring to listen and observe rather than to put myself forward to be heard and seen.

Gretchen was in her element. She glowed. With her husband at her side, and lovingly so, I should say, she beamed with rapid conversation and giddy laughter. If it could be possible, I thought that she seemed all the more confident, and knowing herself and her own opinions, than I had ever before seen. It was as if her husband gave her added strength and even more confidence than usual. This fact (which was obvious to me) made me think upon myself and my own confidence, and in contrast to a woman with a loving husband, how I had been so terribly diminished by my horrid husband over time. With the right kind of husband, I could have been so much more than I was.

With effervescently joyful Gretchen before me, I could not but smile. Seeing the joy of my friend and the bond she was blessed with in her husband, I had to smile in happiness for her. So this was what marriage could be. This was what a good husband could do for a good woman. And so this was marital bliss. I was only an observer to it, but I could feel the radiant happiness exuding from the pair across the table.

As I smiled for the wedded joy of my friend, I felt eyes watching me. I could not help but look over to see Frederick's eyes fixed upon my face. I might have instinctively looked away in a type of embarrassment, but instead, I intensified my smile and smiled *at* Frederick. He haltingly smiled at me in return. And then we both looked away from each other, me a little flushed at my slight boldness, and I thought perhaps he felt a similar kind of discomfiture.

I composed myself. I told myself that, just as Gretchen had said, I could be Frederick's type of sister. Not a close sister, mind you, but a kind of sister to him, through and around Gretchen anyway. I could befriend him just a little without crossing over into any impropriety or temptation for me. He needed drawing out, after all. He needed to believe again. Like his sister thought, I felt that he needed to free himself for love and marriage to a lovely young woman. I could help in that worthy cause on Frederick's behalf, and to aid my friend Gretchen as well. Frederick's happiness would be Gretchen's happiness too.

And so, throughout the rest of the meal and the evening visiting, I freed myself to relax a good deal and to be a friendly kind of sister to Frederick. I did not stop myself from pulling him out of his shell of shyness and engaging him in conversation. I began about music. His face awakened to discuss music.

I even dared to ask him about that song, the one that I had long called my own song (to myself, anyway), "Frederick. There is a melody, and harmony: a song that I have oft heard you play. I would call it hauntingly beautiful. Even melancholy, all the while it is also joyful. That is how it speaks to me, anyway. I was just wondering if you composed it or if someone else did. I was wondering about that particular favorite of mine."

He only looked at me, with a curious brow, obviously having no idea which of his many songs I might mean to ask about. I felt silly that I had expected him to imagine which piece I had meant.

I tried to assist him in recalling the tune, "I am far too shy to hum it to you, and I doubt that my humming would help at all anyhow, but perhaps I could pick a few key notes out on the piano to aid you in knowing which song I mean to inquire about?"

He motioned to the piano nearby. I would never have asked such a thing if my suggestion had meant that we go would upstairs to *his* piano, you understand. The family piano was just sitting near, conveniently, with everyone else around us, and I had meant to pluck out my meager attempt at his song there. We both walked over to it. I sat down on the piano bench and began to play. Of course, I had played this piece, his song, or what I had come to call *my* song, many times in the church. At least, I had tried to recall it to the best of my ability and musical memory. I had done fairly well, I had thought, though I had never imagined in my wildest dreams that I would ever try to play it in front of the musician!

And now, there I was, playing my relatively feeble attempt at that song with the musician standing next to me, watching and listening. You might think that I thought I might die of mortification at the situation, but I am happy to report that I did hold my own very well. I suppose it was all the practice. I had played, or at least tried to play, that song so many times that it came to me easily now. I had practiced enough that I could even put some genuine feeling into it too. I wasn't just plucking notes painfully. I was playing quite confidently. Though my rendition could not possibly compare to his, at least I thought it could remind him of the musical number I was trying to refer him to.

When I was done my own try at his song, Frederick smiled graciously and said, "Oh, yes. I know the one that you mean."

I stood up and boldly requested, "Would you play for me, I mean for *us*, now? Could you play the entire song? I would like to watch, you know, to see how terribly I have recalled that little portion of it."

Frederick smiled once more. "Not at all, I assure you. You played it quite nicely."

Gretchen interjected, "Oh yes, I *love* that one. You did very well with it, Isabelle: a good deal better than I ever could have. Yes, you must play it for us, Frederick."

I had to ask him, "Is it yours? Is it your own composition? I have never heard it before, you see, and I wondered if you composed it."

"Yes. I composed it."

I reiterated my hope, "Please, will you play it for us now?"

"Certainly."

With that, Frederick sat down and began to play. I can tell you, I was rapidly in raptures. My eyes were filled with tears of joy at the privilege of standing there, watching that song being played for me, or at least at my behest. My heart was filled with the pure beauty of that piece of music. I wanted to take a nearby seat and close my wetted eyes to entirely drink it in, but I simply stood, and tried to focus on the notes that his fingers touched, through the veil of my happy tears. I did my utmost to check any further welling of water in my eyes, and I dared not blink or the salty droplets would have been squeezed out to very visibly fall down upon my cheeks.

34
A Blessing, Heaven Sent

As Gretchen's time of confinement was nearing an end, and she and her husband were becoming more and more thrilled at the prospect of their baby, I suddenly realized that I needed to piece together a quilt for the new boy or girl of that joyful event. I wasn't in the habit of having friends who were having babies, but I knew that I must make something beautiful for the first baby of this, my dearest friend. I also wanted to make or do something wonderful for Gretchen.

And so as Gretchen and her husband worked on choosing names, be it predominantly for boys or for girls I could not say for certain; I set to work on the most beautiful baby quilt that I could imagine and muster. Over a length of time, I had become rich in small pieces of quality cloth, for I always saved lovely leftovers that had a way of coming my way amid the process of sewing things for other people, and of course, for my children and myself. No, I had not done a great deal of seamstressing (not nearly as much as I would have liked to), but I had done enough to amass a good deal of glorious scraps of fabric.

My children enjoyed helping me choose which pieces of material to incorporate for the new baby's quilt, and they also enjoyed chatting entertainingly to me as I planned, pieced and sewed it. Once the quilt was basically done, and though beautiful it already was, I decided to add some special embroidery work to it. I could not simply stitch the quilting in ordinary fashion, for I found that I must do something more extraordinary than that. When finally entirely done, I thought it was a singular work of art, though I say it myself.

Lorna and Alan thought the quilt beautiful and even Grandmother Ramstock offered a 'magnificent work' regarding my efforts and the eventual result. I was enraptured that I could give such a worthy gift to my friend for her baby. Before I set to work on it, I had not imagined that it would end so glorious to behold. The quilt had seemed to have a way of letting me know what to do to it along the way of its creation.

With the quilt for Gretchen's baby completed, I set my mind to whatever I might be able to make for my friend. Anything I thought to sew for Gretchen to wear seemed inadequate. Mr. Jennings could afford to dress his wife beautifully enough. I could not compete with any of that, for her wardrobe was gleaned from out east and even some from Europe, I surely thought.

I contemplated petit point and other embroidered items, but I could not settle on anything that would be perfect for the occasion. I finally decided to simply bake something delicious the first day that I would visit to see the baby, and take that over with some of the special preserves I had had a hand in making recently. I could bake, after all. I knew many delicious recipes. I had helped my mother Ramstock put together some wonderful preserves of late. Yes, I would share of our kitchen efforts. '*That* should please my friend Gretchen', I thought. She would be hungry after her travail was behind her, after all.

The day did come. I did not take my children with me that first day, but when the time was deemed appropriate, my little ones were thrilled to go see Gretchen's new baby. Gretchen had been delighted to receive the quilt for her beautiful new baby boy, even as she enjoyed my gifts from the elder Mrs. Ramstock's kitchen.

When I first talked to my friend turned new mother, she was beaming, "Is he not the most beautiful baby you have ever seen?"

I answered thusly, "With such handsome parents, how could he not be beautiful?"

"Well, I know that I am partial towards him, being that I love him more than I could ever before imagine loving anyone. Do all mothers feel this way, Isabelle?"

"I would think so. I should hope so."

"Oh, I know that you love your own babies more than mine, but still, do you not agree that he is perfectly angelic? Do you not instantly love him too?"

"To love the mother is to love the child. How could I help but love him too, Gretchen, for he is *your* baby."

The little new Jennings fellow was named after his father, Douglas, and also named after his uncle and grandfather Weiss, in Douglas Frederick. Yes, Douglas Frederick Jennings seemed to have a nice ring to it, we all thought. The name did seem to suit his little darling face. I thought I could even imagine the handsome young man of some future day in those tiny features.

I thoroughly enjoyed taking my turns holding Gretchen's little boy each time I went to visit and Lorna thrilled in helping cradle him. Alan thought that little Douglas was taking too long to get up and play with him. Why wouldn't he simply begin to walk and talk yet, after all? Alan fancied Douglas to become his play partner. He was a boy too, you see.

It was decided between Gretchen and her husband, with a determined Mrs. Weiss hinting heartily in the background, that the three now Jennings family should stay at some length. Mrs. Weiss had convinced her daughter that for safety's sake, it was best to keep the new baby boy where he was, until he was a good deal larger and stronger. A new baby should not embark upon especially extensive travels, all agreed. Gretchen's son would not be considered fit for a long and arduous trip for at least a few months to come, and then, the Jennings three could return to their home in the east.

Mrs. Weiss was happy to keep her daughter and grandson in the house a little longer, and Gretchen was happier to stay with her mother than to go home to be near her mother-in-law. I thought it pitiable that Gretchen did not have the likes of my own mother-in-law. And, by the same sort of token, Gretchen certainly pitied me that I was not blessed with a good husband. She was certainly grateful for her husband, and a good husband can surely make up for a lesser mother-in-law. Yes, I guessed that Gretchen loved her husband almost as much as his namesake, their beloved son. The youngest Douglas Jennings currently reigned supreme in her heart.

35
The Gulf

Since Gretchen had her baby, I had visited a little. Not so much as my daughter would have liked, though, for Lorna was enamored with the idea of a baby. She loved to help hold little Douglas. Nevertheless, I wanted to avoid robbing Gretchen of any sleep that she might be able to get. Yes, I fancied at first that I could go over and hold her baby while she rested or caught up on much needed sleep, but Gretchen could not seem to attempt such repose whenever I came to call. She must get herself lively and visit with me. She could not help talking to me if I were in the house. She explained that her mother and others in the house thoroughly enjoyed caring for little Douglas whenever she wanted solitude or slumbers.

Thus, I kept my visits to the Weiss house minimal to allow Gretchen opportunities for extra sleeping, and I visited only as much as I thought that Gretchen wished her friend over for chatting. I tended to wait for an invitation. I was never inclined to overstay my welcome with anyone in any event, and I never wished to be an unwelcome intrusion in the least measure. This was illustrative of my reserved nature, I suppose.

Another consideration was that I did not want to keep Gretchen from her husband, who currently seemed like a fish out of water: he was not used to the leisurely life and lulling excesses of an old world gentleman. He was in the habit of working. The little I saw of Mr. Douglas Jennings was enough to convince me that he was having some difficulty with his present resting and retiring state of non-affairs. He paced about. He could not sit for long. He shifted and fidgeted in his chair whenever he did sit at all. Consequently, I thought that I should not take his sweet wife from him. I thought it very good for Gretchen, her husband and their little baby boy, to have plenty of time just to themselves.

Beyond leaving my dear friend to her husband and new child, I wished to mainly stay away from the Weiss home with another needful purpose in mind. I held more than one reason for avoiding the piano house. I told myself that there was a personal temptation for me there. Yes, it was the musician. I was drawn to Frederick and I could not allow myself to be attracted to him in any way. I simply should not approach that indulgence in any form or fashion.

Though I had been in the musician's house a number of times of late, I had not really spoken to him since he had played his song for me that night we first actually had met. I could not. I dared not. Though I might sometimes imagine that I could be as a sister and friend to him, I thought the better of such a concept or the attempt. The line that would need to be drawn was too sketchy a one. Where would I stand as sisterly friend? How far away? How close could I dare to get? No, upon reflection, I generally thought I could not even allow myself to be Frederick's friend at all.

Gretchen would have liked Frederick and me to be friends. Somehow she thought that I could settle right in beside her as his other sister. She was still an innocent in many ways, I thought. Naïve, perhaps: yes, it was naïve of Gretchen to think that I could sit and talk with Frederick just as she could, without generating improper feelings towards him. I was married, and I could not forget that fact, no matter how much I might desperately wish to. I already felt an attraction to Frederick and, inadvertently, I had already entered dangerous territory with respect to him.

Perhaps Frederick would never be attracted to me in any romantic way. Maybe *he* was safe to simply be my brotherly friend. I did not know his mind and heart, at least especially relating to me. It was entirely quite possible that Frederick's heart was perfectly safe where I was concerned. However, I knew myself enough to

know that my own heart was not safe near the musician. I had
fallen in love with his music, his songs, my song, our song, and I
would never be safe near him now. My heart was surely not safe.
I had met the man. I thought that I had begun to like the man as
much as his music. I knew that I was drawn to Frederick as much
as I was to his music. He *was* his music, to me.

Maybe I could not delineate the line between the musician
and the man. Perhaps I was only enamored by the songs and
therefore I was childishly or romantically enraptured by the man
who composed and played them. It was possible in time that I
would find that I loved the music but not the man. Still, I was not
at liberty to find out any of those kinds of details. I had no right to
such territory. I was held strictly under my marital vows.

My secret thoughts surrounding the musician filled too
much of my mind. I struggled to crowd them out. I had not been
working lately. With all the goings-on at the Weiss house, I had
not hinted for any work and Mrs. Weiss had not pressed me for
any either. I assumed that Mrs. Weiss was entirely revolving around
Gretchen and the new baby, not to mention Mr. Douglas Jennings
and his company as well. I supposed that my more idle hands were
part of my problem. I wondered if I should garner work again.

However, I could not bring myself to take in washing again just
yet. I had been spoiled. I only wanted to do needlework. However,
this kind of more pleasant work was not prevalent in our territory.
I could easily find more than enough laundering work to keep
me busier than I could keep up with. It was much hard work for
very little pay. In contrast, there was occasional easy seamstressing
work for a little better pay. For the time being, I decided to take
on whatever sewing jobs that I could round about. I would work a
little now and then, get commensurate compensation in coin, and
focus the rest of my energies on guiding my two angelic children. It
was surely time to begin teaching Lorna to read. I told myself that I
must halt my thoughts regarding the musician.

I cannot think of Frederick. I have manufactured a gulf
between us. If he could ever think of me in the way that I feel that

I could think of him, I know we cannot explore what could be. I can barely think of the word: together. I should not even walk by his piano house to hear him playing. My life must be devoid of his music. I can only play for myself. I still had the piano at the church, after all. But how could I play that song? Such a thing would be too painful to me at present.

36
Bloodied

He barely made it home that night. He could hardly stay on his good and faithful horse. He was hunched over like a one-hundred year old man, I thought. He had terrible trouble standing on his own and likely could not have made it up the stairs to his room. The Ramstock servants helped him up to his bed. I felt quite shocked at seeing my husband thusly. I could not but feel pity and compassion for him, not that I suddenly loved him again (as his wife), but only that I felt empathy for him as a fellow human being.

The doctor came right away. When he came out of my husband's room, he told us all that we must prepare ourselves. The young Mr. Ramstock might only have days to live. We must make him comfortable, we were told. The doctor gave us medicines to help him rest and feel less pain. There was an internal infection that seemed to be growing. The bullet had been removed, but the infection in his stomach would not likely recede. Yes, a miracle of healing was always possible, but there was essentially nothing human to be done. Besides the mustard poultice that the elder Mrs. Ramstock prepared for her son and insisted could surely help, nature would be left to take its course. Only Heaven could truly save the man if it was God's will. Prayers were suggested. Even the parson came to give what comforts he could.

The next morning came soon. As my husband requested, I brought our children to his bedside. He seemed as if deathbed repentant about not having been much of a father to them. It was obvious to me that he was harboring plenty of regrets. At one point, he even reached out to grasp my hand. I could not deny him that. I looked upon him with great pity in my heart.

I did not ask him each and all of what had happened. The little he had said told me enough. He had been gambling in a little town nearby. He was accused of cheating at cards. He did not then admit to that sort of deceit to me, nor before to the men at the gambling table, I was certain. I supposed that it was a moot point now, anyway. Right there in the saloon, my husband's accuser had shot him almost point blank: from across the table, anyway. Whether a just punishment in the least or not at all, the bullet was instant judge and jury, I suppose you could say.

My husband did not look himself at all, lying in his bed. He was obviously suffering, both from injury and infection. He was feverish, shivering, groaning and sweating. He had insisted on more liquor than his mother thought would be good for him, but she did wish to mask his pain in any way that she could help to do. I thought I saw terror, or at least a good deal of fear written on his face. I had never seen my husband this way or anything close to it. He had always been a robustly healthy man, and was still a very young one.

When my children had gone off with their grandmother for a time, my husband began lamenting to me, "I am *dying*, Isabelle. I am dying for certain. I know it. You know it too, don't you?"

I tried to be of help, "I *don't* know it. The bullet has been removed. You have an infectious fever. You could certainly rally *still*. Rest. Be still. Hope and believe. What do doctors know? They have been wrong before. Sleep if you can. Let your body heal itself. Perhaps you will feel more yourself by tomorrow, and every day you might become better and better."

"Perhaps. But, I fear that I *am* dying. I *truly* do."

"Do your best to believe that you will live. Rest, sleep and hope towards tomorrow. You may begin to feel well by then. Think on the future. Believe you will live."

He looked like a frightened little boy as he haltingly expressed, "Isabelle? But, if I die, am I going to hell, do you think? I feel like I am already there. Do you think there is forgiveness in the next life for me? Do you think that God will forgive me for the things I have done wrong in my life?"

I felt compassion but I could not lie, "I cannot pass judgment like that. But, I do believe that God is a fair Father, and a loving one too."

He sighed, moaned and tried to shift towards more comfort in his bed. I sat there next to him, saying nothing while holding his hand just as he wished me to. I tried to say such things that would comfort his mind whenever he seemed to want me to. I knew that he was suffering as much in spirit as he was in body. I knew that he was terrified to die and to meet his Maker. His mind was wracked in torment, I thought. I could not feel great confidence that my wayward husband would not spend a little time in hell whenever it was that he might finally die, but he was no murderer. He had done plenty of wrong against me, but he had never murdered anyone. I felt assured that the man who shot him was far more likely to suffer at length in hell for what he had done to my husband.

Several days pained by. I spent much of my time at my husband's side, my children coming and going, and the elder Mrs. Ramstock also taking her turn at her son's bedside. The senior Mr. Ramstock had been called for, and when he arrived, he also took his turns by the sickbed. Both my husband's parents wore their worries outwardly. This was their one son, their one child. I could see the devastation that they felt at the prospect of losing their only son. There were many tears spent for their boy. It was clear that neither of them wished to lose him so soon in this life.

Each night that passed further diminished any hopes that the younger Mr. Ramstock would live. He was not doing any better day upon day. He was not rallying. His parents kept calling for the doctor, hoping that something new could be tried. New medicines were attempted. He continued very ill. He seemed to be simply slipping away, and nothing could be done to save him from his untimely end. No prayers, no tears, no hopes and no wishes changed what was to be.

37
Free to Choose

Black is all my wardrobe these days. I cannot say what I feel. It is a mix of things, I suppose. Even though I feel a definite type of sorrow, I do feel a certain sense of relief. I can not wish my husband living, with me at least, necessarily, but I do not truly wish him still dead. I suppose I am all a jumble. I think most of what I feel, to begin with, is a profound sadness for the life my husband chose to live and the life that he could have lived instead. I can imagine such better things than the path which he preferred to trod down.

I would be lying to suggest that my heart aches for my husband. I do not miss him. His absence seems a normal thing, though I know he will never return in this life to his parents' home. I had long since wished *not* to be his wife. I would have preferred a divorce to his death, of course, if that could have been possibly accomplished. I would have rather that my husband lived and improved himself and his life. I suppose if he would have done that, I might have been able to eventually find happiness as his wife. But that is of no account now. He is dead.

I pity his parents. I especially feel the sorrows of his mother. I cannot say what his father deserved, but I surely know that *she* never deserved such unhappiness. She must have been as wonderful a mother as she is a grandmother. I do not know about the father, but I do know the mother well. I have tried to be of what comfort I can to her, but mostly I have encouraged my children to give their grandmother far more embraces than usual. I think that is helping.

My mother-in-law seems to melt into their arms. I know that
she feels their love, and that is more medicine than anything else
could be to her. I will continually teach my children to honor their
grandmother Ramstock.

The elder Mr. Ramstock kept to his room a great deal after the
funeral. His wife did the same at first, but then she ventured out
more and more. Her grandchildren seemed the best comfort to her,
but there seemed nothing to comfort Mr. Ramstock. It seemed a
little strange or curious to me that a man, a father, who had seemed
so distant where his son was concerned, would be so terribly
sorrowed by the untimely death of his son.

Prior to the death of my husband, I might have imagined that
his father did not love him at all, or at least very much, but the
overwhelming devastation that I see in the father since, has caused
me to rethink what he felt for his son all along. It is clear to me
now that he loved him very much. I only could not see it before,
and quite sadly, I should say that the son never knew that his father
so fully loved him either. I cannot help but think now, what a
difference it could have made in my husband's life and character,
if he had known that his father loved him. Perhaps he would have
been more of a husband to me and a better father to our children.

But all this was surmising. Though I might be inclined to think
at length about what could have been, there was not much point to
only thinking such thoughts. What good would it do me to ponder
excessively about all the things that might have been? I wondered if
perhaps I should think about what was to be from now on. What
would become of me and my children?

There was no question of my moving out and becoming
destitute or anything of that sort. No, Grandmother Ramstock
wanted my children with her and therefore I would still be
welcome in her house for many years to come. As the mother of
her grandchildren, I was a part of her family. And with her son
gone forevermore, she felt the need of family all the more. She had
no children living now, and my children were her life's blood and
greatest reason for living, I felt.

However, I was still young. I was not unattractive, though I say it myself. I was a young widow now. I would be considered marriageable by some men, young or older. I was aware of at least a number of eligible prospects in the territory for a single woman. Some of those men would certainly not be opposed to marrying a young widow. I knew that I should not consider remarriage for at least an acceptable mourning period of time, but did I want to think of marriage again at all? I feared another bad choice. Could I be sure of my own wisdom in choosing another life's partner? Should I trust myself in this? I hoped that I had learned from my past mistake.

Of course, I confess that my mind began wandering towards the piano house once more. I could not but think of the musician from time to time. My mind was sometimes fixed on Frederick. I could not help it.

Now I was free, but would the musician care? I was fairly assured that Gretchen might hint at her brother towards thinking on marriage to me. I thought she would like that outcome, even excessively. But what Gretchen might like was not necessarily what her brother would hope for or agree to. Who knew Frederick's heart and wishes? Would he possibly pursue me in any way now that I was free to choose another husband? I thought that wasn't likely, at least in the immediate future.

Firstly, as I have just said, there was the obligatory mourning period of time on my part. It would seem shameful of me, around the county wide, if I leaned towards marriage to another man too soon. Secondly, Frederick was not inclined to marry again; and if he should begin to lean towards marrying again, why should I be so bold as to assume that he would even consider *me*? Was he even attracted to me in such a way, at all? I knew that I was attracted to his music, at least. But was he to be *my* musician? That was quite another question.

38
A Chance Meeting

With Mr. Ramstock senior still keeping mostly to his room and Grandmother Ramstock needing my children at her side, I began to feel the need to get out and walk. I did not feel much required in the Ramstock house at present. I knew that my children were quite able to help their grandmother's heart heal, and so I thought to take myself off by myself, beyond my room, and my children's rooms. I knew that a long walk would do me good.

Yes, I had been in the garden a good deal. I had been walking the Ramstock property day after day, and week upon week. Still, this was only walking round and round and I began to feel like a caged wild animal. I craved stretching my legs far beyond the Ramstock yard. There was a favorite wooded path of mine not far from the Ramstock home that I sometimes sauntered onto. It was a place that few besides me seemed to stray into. It was a path that I could reasonably be assured of being alone, at least for the most of the while that I might choose to walk there.

This time there, I had walked that length of path in solitary style, back and forth for at least an hour, I was sure. Not a person had stepped onto it to disturb me. It was now late in the afternoon and no eye or ear was anywhere near to watch or hear me. For some reason even unknown to myself, I began to instinctively sigh. It was as if I needed to breathe out some past tensions of life. There had been many anxious events and moments of late, and I had greatly felt the strain of them. I breathed in and out deeply at length. The walking and breathing had a cathartically healing effect upon me.

Each turn back and forth on the path seemed to afford me more and more relaxation. I felt freer and freer of life's former cares, in a way. I began to feel a little happiness that I had not recalled much in quite some time. Without thinking, I began to hum a little. The little turned to more. Soon I was humming a tune in earnest. I did not know which melody at first, but then I realized it was *that* song. I gave myself to it. Why not? It had become *my* song. Yes, it was Frederick's song first, but I had long since come to own it too.

I became somewhat oblivious to anything around me. I did not care if the birds heard me humming. They sang their own songs, did they not? And what did they care if I heard them singing? I would be as a bird, I told myself. I would freely hum, and then I tried whistling. I attempted the melody in a whistle as I walked along that path. I was almost as if marching as I stretched my legs and swung my arms, whistling the song of the musician. I felt joy. I was as if in the clouds, flying, a bird with wings.

At the end of the path once more, I had turned about to walk the length again, singing still as I went. In actuality, I was alternating in humming and whistling, half wishing I could put worthy words to the melody. After my number of steps forward, a twig snapped just behind me. The noise was unmistakable. I sharply turned around to see who had joined me on the path. I was pleasantly surprised to see the musician.

Gretchen's brother looked as if he had just been caught stealing a cookie from the family jar. I was startled, but not enough to prevent my smiling at the look on Frederick's face. I stopped myself. Perhaps he had something serious or foreboding to tell me. We both stood there frozen in time, staring at each other. I briefly awaited his pronouncement. Had he come looking for me to tell me of some bad news regarding Gretchen or her baby? My head wanted to swim with possible worries. I stopped myself again. I realized that maybe Frederick was only out for a walk, just as I was. But why would he have come walking so far? This path was near the Ramstock house, not near the Weiss house.

Rather than letting my mind run wild with wondering, and without much thinking, I asked, "Were you looking for someone, or something?"

He faltered of speech and then gathered himself to say in return, "No, I only was out walking and then came upon this path."

I smiled. "I find myself here often. It is a favorite quiet place for me to walk. Few others ever tread it."

"I have never walked exactly here before. I heard you singing, I think?"

I blushed and felt the full embarrassment of having been heard singing his composition, at least doing it such an injustice was what I feared, and so I thought to say, "Oh, dear. I was humming and whistling your song. I am sorry if I have usurped it in any way unpleasant to you."

"No, no, not at all. I followed the song on the wind. It brought me here."

My face was still flushed with redness. I tried to shake my blushing off by changing focus away from Frederick's song and my having been humming and whistling it, "You have never walked here on this path before?"

"No, though it seems a very pleasant place to walk."

"A perfect place for some solitude."

He suddenly looked a little more uncomfortable than he had prior, "Yes. I am sorry. Have I disturbed you, in your solitude? Would you like me to leave you alone to your walking?"

I suddenly felt aware of his discomfort, "Oh no, not at all, I assure you. I have more than enough solitude whenever I want it."

We were still standing, facing each other. I secretly wished we were walking together instead; but I did not quite know how to suggest that. I began thinking on what I might say to change this slightly awkward stance, into walking side by side.

Frederick seemed to be thinking in line with me, for he offered, "May I walk with you here a while, then?"

I was quite delighted, "Oh yes, please, let us walk."

As we began strolling along together, he said, "I have heard of your loss. I hope you, your children, and your parents-in-law are feeling some comforts in your sorrow?"

I could not honestly speak of my own loss and sorrow, or even that of my children, and so I thought to say only, "My parents-in-law feel their loss keenly."

"Yes, I am sure that they do."

I only nodded.

Frederick continued, "Gretchen told me of the funeral, that it was a nice service, and that she spoke to you there."

I could only muster, "Yes."

Very plainly he spoke these words, "Sometimes life deals us ungenerously."

I looked at him and into his eyes, for he was looking exactly at me. I wondered what he was trying to say to me. I wanted to say many things. I felt assured that Gretchen must have told him most things that she knew about me and my marriage. I was certain that he suspected that I knew a great deal about him. But what could I say at such a time? Nothing. I could not say anything it seemed. The right words escaped me, I feared to say something the wrong way, and so I said nothing for the moment.

He looked away. We walked along silently: a good many steps on the path.

Before too much time elapsed after his last words, and having had a short while to ponder a little, I attempted, "Yes, life is seldom what we expected that it would be, I should say. When we are young, we are full of hope and faith, and then, too often for many of us perhaps, through no fault of our own, our hopes are dashed and our faith falters."

He looked at me again, and with some intensity of feeling, he only said, "Yes."

I thought aloud, "Victims of circumstance, I suppose we could say."

Again, he said, "Yes."

I felt to add as a question, "But, we should only look back to check our own mistakes, and try to look forward all the more?"

Frederick looked thoughtful, and then agreed by elucidating, "We can learn from our own history, determine not to repeat our mistakes, but not let the actions of others nor past pains cripple us from forging forward. The past does not determine our futures."

I smiled. "Yes, we can choose another path."

He smiled in return, nodding, "Yes. Past sorrows do not keep us from future happiness."

I thought in that moment that I had not seen Frederick smile very often. He seemed quite the more handsome fellow to me when he smiled.

He surprised me with, "Isabelle?"

"Yes?"

"I must confess something to you."

"Yes? What is it?" I was all the more surprised.

"Please forgive me for being so very forward, but I must tell you something. I have been disingenuous. I must be entirely honest with you. I walked out here near your home on purpose to find you today. Gretchen told me of your favorite places to go walking on your own. I have walked near here many days hoping to find you. And then today, I heard you humming and whistling my tune. I cannot tell you how happy I felt to hear you. Forgive me, but I wanted to see and talk to you. I could think of no other way than to keep coming around here. I have been thinking about you of late, you understand."

I was completely taken aback. I had not known Frederick to be forward in any way before. This seemed unprecedented to me. What was I to say? I knew not what to say. I instantly hoped for a little courage. Had not Frederick exercised a good deal of courage to say what he had just said to me? I could not leave him wanting by saying nothing. I wanted to encourage him.

He had been looking at me but had looked away again.

I mustered, "I have been thinking of you as well."

He turned again and smiled at me. "As you can imagine, Gretchen has been speaking a great deal about you to me. All the more so just lately, you know, much more than she did before."

I fully smiled up into his face, "Yes, I can well imagine."

He laughed. "I am sure that you can picture her acting as a matchmaker, now, you know, between us."

I think I giggled a little and then agreed, "Undoubtedly, now that you mention the idea."

We both shared laughter at the prospect of Gretchen's efforts on our behalf. I could not help it, knowing Gretchen as I did, and obviously, Frederick knew his sister all the better and so chuckled along with me. We smiled a good while as we continued walking side by side on my favorite wooded pathway. Now and then I glanced over at my walking companion. I wanted to look at him far more than I did. I caught his gaze as he looked over at me from time to time. I could not help but thrill within.

We talked a little as we walked a great deal. I was too happy to speak much, and either Frederick was a man of few words, as I certainly and fully suspected, or he felt very much the same as I did while the early evening overtook us. The sinking sun created a beautiful painting surrounding us as we strolled together.

39
A Duet

Gretchen had invited me to dine again at the Weiss home. I did my best to diminish the event to my mother-in-law. I did not like her to suspect my growing feelings for Frederick and his apparent attractions towards me. I proposed my going over to see Gretchen and her baby, letting my mother Ramstock think it simply an evening's visit with my friend and her new child rather than an afternoon one. Instead of accompanying me as would be usual in a morning or afternoon appointment, my children would be lovingly cared for and tucked into bed by their grandmother, and I would be given the horse and buggy once again for my evening out and away from home.

My feelings this time were so very different from my last evening of dinner and delights in the Weiss home. My heart was not cloistered now. I was free to feel. I could truly be the still young woman that I was, rather than what I forcibly suppressed myself into before. No, I would not talk and laugh with wild abandon. It was not exactly in my nature to do so anyway. I would remain quite reserved. I imagined that all would outwardly look very much as before, this time. The Weiss family would generally see me no differently. Still, there would be a marked difference going on in my mind and heart. I would let myself love Frederick as much as I thought that he was feeling a kind of warmth for me, and as much as I believed he deserved.

Gretchen was all effervescence. The joy in her heart was visibly apparent. It was obvious that she wanted to play swift matchmaker to her brother and me. She sat us together: before, during and after the lovely meal. She did her utmost to engage Frederick and myself in conversation. Indeed, she tried so hard to get the two of us talking to each other together that she dominated the dialogue in a way. It seemed quite comical to me. She was darling in her efforts. I thought I saw her husband raise an eyebrow and sigh a time or two. I suspected he felt Gretchen far too overt in her plans.

I watched Mr. and Mrs. Weiss a good deal, wondering what they thought of the goings on, and I could not exactly guess what either might be feeling. I had always gathered that Mrs. Weiss was inclined to like me, but would she continue to like me now that she might suspect that I was attracted to her reclusive son? I could never know what Mr. Weiss thought of me, but would he like me more or less now that Gretchen was making a match between Frederick and me possible? Before, I was no threat to everything staying the same for them, but now, now I could change everything in the Weiss household. I was certain that both parents must be thinking something along these lines. I was a widow with two children, after all. If I were to marry their son, obviously either my children would move into their house with me, or Frederick would move out to live somewhere else with me and my little ones. I could not imagine what Frederick's parents' hearts were feeling surrounding such prospects.

Such thoughts helped keep me quite reserved, I suppose. I was my generally quiet self. I did not put myself forward unless I felt fully compelled. I left most of the talking to Gretchen, and I dare say that I talked even less than Frederick did. As he intermittently became somewhat animated in his part of any conversation, I sometimes glanced over at especially his mother to see her reaction. I thought that she perhaps enjoyed seeing him so felicitous, like I did. It was a joyful thing to behold. A happy Frederick was so delightfully different than a reticent one. Refreshingly wonderful, I thought, quite truthfully.

Likely in an effort to draw me out and also to get Frederick and I sealed together in cheerfulness, Gretchen suddenly proposed,

"Isabelle, I wonder if you would indulge me? I wonder if you would consent to trying out a duet or two with my brother."

Frederick looked as surprised and perhaps self-conscious at the proposal as I felt: Gretchen had obviously not consulted him prior to her suggestion. In any other situation, I could have been fairly easily prevailed upon to play piano for a little gathering of friends or family members such as this, at least since having practiced at the piano so many times of late. However, to play for and with Frederick seemed too daunting a task to me. Not only was he a master musician and a genius at the piano, but my heart was wrapped up in thoughts of falling in love with him. To sit beside him and to try to play any duet with him seemed overwhelming to say the least. I thought I dared not play. I was nervous beyond explanation. I wondered what I might say to get out of it. I did not wish to insult anyone in the room, but I feared to play the piano in this way, this night.

As Frederick and I exchanged agape looks, Gretchen pressed further, "Please say that you will, Isabelle? Frederick? It would delight me more than anything at present. You will comply with your dear sister's one special wish for this evening, won't you, my brother? You will help Isabelle if she falters in the least?"

I could not but love Gretchen for her herculean efforts. I knew exactly all that she was about and I could not fault her one jot for embarrassing me thusly. She meant well. For all the discomfort I might be feeling, I knew that my darling friend meant very well. She only wanted to help us along. She only wanted to make us fall for each other. She simply wished for us to marry, and to bring happiness to ourselves as well as to her. I daresay that she thought my marriage to her brother would bring happiness to all in the house. I hoped at such an idea, but I was not so certain as my friend.

Frederick rose and came to the aid of at least me, putting out his hand towards me while he smiled and offered, "Isabelle? Come. Let us sit together and see what we can do. You can teach me your favorite duet and then I can teach you mine. Let us start *there* at least. Do not think of this as a performance. Let us simply have a jolly time of it, and the more fun that we have at it, the more everyone in the room will be entertained."

How could I refuse that? I deeply wanted to decline the offer, to save myself fumbling at the piano in front of everyone and especially Frederick, but then again, I was thrilled at the prospect of playing with him. What a mix of feelings. My desires were juxtaposed to say the least. I relented, with as gracious a smile as I could muster. I tried not to allow my weakened knees to dominate me. I attempted to rally my courage. I wanted to enjoy the experience. It seemed a rare experience, indeed.

Once seated at the piano together, we did begin with me teaching the best duet I knew to Frederick. If he knew the piece already, he gave me the courtesy of not allowing me to know. Of course he was a quick study, as if he must have already known it, but he was thoroughly gentlemanlike in the process. Once we had played my little duet choice together a few times, he showed me some notes that I could easily add to make the song that much the richer. He also added a good deal of notes to his side of the tune. Why should I be surprised at these melodically harmonic additions? No, I was not surprised, but I was completely enthralled with delight in the midst of it.

My duet gave way to his choice of a number. I was pleasantly surprised to learn that he was making it easy for me. It was not anything difficult to play as I had feared he might present me with. It was an easy enough piece, at least the melodious part that he showed me to play. His side of the duet was far more complex, as I quickly saw. We played that one until I knew my part of the duet well, at least for this night. I could not be assured that I would remember it by tomorrow. I was not the musical wonder that Frederick was.

Several duets later, Frederick having shown me what easy thing I could play, and then his having added the bulk of the melody, the room was awash in enjoyment. I knew that I was certainly enjoying myself, and I thought that so was everyone else. Who could not enjoy such piano playing? Of course, I speak not of my part in the music, but of what magic the fingers of the musician conjured.

40
Cupid's Attempts

Gretchen's husband had dropped her by the Ramstock house for a relatively quick call upon me. Their little but growing baby Douglas was home with his doting Grandmother Weiss. Once I had met Gretchen at the door and assured her that I could take a few turns around the Ramstock gardens with her, she waved her husband away with a smile. It was a lovely day for a walking conversation and my two children were reading with their grandmother anyway. We two friends were shortly outside.

Gretchen briefly took one of my hands in hers before lamenting, "My dearest Isabelle. These past months have swept by and I have hardly seen you."

As we began our gentle walking I smiled. "I daresay you have been trying to catch some sleep, when you were not caring for your baby boy."

Her face seemed a little sad. "And soon I will be away and gone, not knowing when I will be back again. I will miss you dearly."

I tried to console, "We will have letters, as much as we wish."

She said only, "Yes."

"And, if I know your mother, she will have you back again before we know it."

"Yes, I suppose. But my husband's mother will not want to let us go any time soon. I am certain that she is thoroughly vexed with us, or at least with *me*, for keeping her from meeting her grandson all this time. You should see her letters to my husband. Quite cross,

I assure you."

"Well, once she has little Douglas in her arms, all will be forgotten. She will think only of him."

She smiled. "Yes, I suppose you are quite right on that count."

"I am certain of it. She will be nothing but in raptures."

Gretchen looked around the yard and then sighed, "You know, I have hardly stepped outside since my baby was born. How the time has flown. I have been a bit of a caged bird."

"Quite the case for many of us. Having a baby is entirely overwhelming in many ways. We have absolutely no idea what we are in for until it happens to us. Becoming a mother is far, far more than we could have ever imagined before."

"Oh yes, that is so very true."

"How much longer do you think your husband can wait before he gets himself back to his work?"

She laughed. "Oh, yes. He is beside himself in frustration waiting, and *waiting* on me as well. He simply cannot wait to leave. He wants to get back as soon as my mother and I will allow it."

"Well, it is wise not to travel until your baby is robustly old enough."

"I had not imagined these details prior to his birth, but yes, I entirely agree with that point. I am glad that my mother is all the more persuasive than me with my husband. She is so very good at being stern when need be. I might have been cajoled into leaving much sooner than might have been best."

I smiled. "Yes, I cannot picture *you* being stern."

She chuckled. "I can become *quite* stern if needs must, I assure you."

"No, I cannot believe it."

"Yes, yes, it is far too true. I am not always the jolly angel that I know you imagine me to be."

"No, Gretchen, do not tarnish my glorious heavenly image of you. I like to think of you as an angel of felicity."

All at once, my children ran out to inquire of Gretchen about her baby and his progress. They adorably complained about not having seen little Douglas in too, too long. Gretchen assured them that they were welcome to come see him any day, and then the begging towards me began. I promised to take them the next day; and then they were off in the yard to pick up sticks and to gather stones to make some little thing of their inventing. I think they were to make mud pies as well. Gretchen and I resumed our stroll.

She leaned in close, confiding, "Frederick and I speak of you a great deal together."

I blushed, said nothing, but nodded with a smile.

"He likes you very much."

I managed, "I like him very much as well. How could I not?"

"I will now confess to you Isabelle, as you might have guessed already, but I have designs to get you and my brother married."

I could not but smile.

She continued, "I might say that I am on the verge of hounding my brother about it. I would like to get you married before I go back, but I fear that is not possible. Frederick is so very reserved. He will need time to work up his courage to ask you. And he would not like me pushing him or asking you *for* him."

I laughed. I could not help it.

She was quite serious, "You laugh, but you know me well enough to believe that I *would* ask you for him, if I thought that would do the trick."

Still smiling, I answered, "Yes, Gretchen, I do believe that you would ask me, *for* your brother. But these things must work themselves out in their own due time. You cannot live and choose for your brother in this way. You cannot and should not compel him in such matters."

She nodded vigorously. "I know, I know. Yes, I know it."

I quickened my step, lilting suddenly. I felt a strange happiness at this amusingly serious conversation.

Gretchen continued, "It frustrates me so! I am certain that you and Frederick are meant to be together. I'm sure that you two should marry. Why not *now*? Right away! I know that you will both be happy together. I only wish to get things right, and on the path as they should be, as soon as may be accomplished. I want it all done before I go back. I fear to leave, and to leave it undone. I do not want anything to go awry. I strongly feel as if I *must* make it happen before I leave for fear of it fading away or falling apart for some strange or sudden reason. I cannot imagine why, but I feel a slight sense of foreboding on the matter. I do not want you and Frederick to lose your chance at love and marriage with each other. I love each of you dearly and I want the both of you to be happy, as happy as I am. I *know* you will be happy together."

I looked at my friend, with all seriousness and boldness beyond my own expectations, "Gretchen, I have been falling in love with your brother. I love him. It is done. If he asked me today, I could not but say yes. Now, he needs to know within himself for certain that he loves me enough to take that leap of faith into marriage again. He should not be rushed. Let him go at his own pace. He needs to feel assured that he loves me enough to marry me, and to take on the fatherhood of my children as well."

Gretchen squeezed my arm with warmth. "That is done, Isabelle. He loves you deeply, I am certain of it. You should see the way he looks when he talks about you. And he feels fondly for your children too."

I smiled with reassurance. "There is time. There is no need to hurry. I am still seen as in mourning anyway. My parents-in-law and the townsfolk would not think too well of me if I was to marry again so suddenly. Perhaps it is best to wait a little while longer, in any event. Give Frederick time to be ready to ask me himself, and give me time to wear black the proper period as a widow. If all this is meant to be, it will all work itself out in due time. Don't fret, Gretchen. And don't keep your poor husband out west here any longer on my and your brother's accounts."

She chuckled at first, and then shared, "I know, I know, but I would so much like to see you both married before I return eastward."

I thought to suggest, "Well, look at it this way, if you leave your brother to take his own due time to finally ask me to marry him, you will have a wedding to come *back* for. See? You would have an excuse to come back for a visit sooner than otherwise."

She smiled. "Yes, yes, perhaps you are right. I must learn patience. It is too true. I cannot have everything that I want the moment that I wish for it."

41
Going Blind?

Gretchen came calling again, a number of days later. It was days after I took my children over to see her baby again, just as I had promised them. Our visit with little Douglas had been a short and yet sweet one. I did not wish to tire anyone out with my boisterous children, and so I took them home again in fairly short order. It was just as well, for they were satisfied with having seen and helped to hold the baby soon enough. They were ready to run home again by the time I thought we were in no danger of over-staying our welcome.

Once Gretchen and I were out of doors in the Ramstock yard, and upon having seated ourselves on a bench together for our chat, she became all seriousness, leaning close to quietly say, "The doctor was over to see Frederick first thing this morning."

I felt a sudden concern, "Oh? Is something the matter? Is he ill? He seemed well enough the few moments I saw him the other day."

"Have I told you of his headaches? Has he told you?"

"No. I have heard nothing of his headaches."

"Well, he has long been prone to headaches. He is used to them, I suppose. He has learned to live with them. He never complains about them, you know. Well, they have been getting far worse and it seems his vision is being affected. He has been having these horrible spells, you see. The headaches even make him feel quite ill and unable to eat, sometimes."

"Oh dear, what did the doctor say?"

Gretchen looked devastated. "He said that if Frederick's

headaches persist, and his eyesight continues to suffer, it might mean that he is going blind."

I was overwhelmed with complete compassion, "Is there nothing that can be done? Does the doctor have any advice? What is Frederick to do?"

Gretchen looked quite frustrated, "Nothing, I suppose. It seems that there is nothing that can be done. We are to wait. We are to wait and see what happens. It could be weeks, months or perhaps even longer before we have an idea if the headaches and his eyesight troubles mean anything foreboding. He could get better, or he could get worse. Perhaps he could stay the same. He could be fine, or he could lose his sight."

"But what will Frederick do? Has the doctor told him to rest, or anything?"

"The doctor doesn't really know anything, I should say. I think he is just guessing, or surmising what is wrong and what could happen. I want Frederick to come east with us to see other doctors who might know more about his condition, but he refuses. He says he simply wants to continue with his composing and what will be, will be. I am terribly worried about him, I can tell you."

"Oh yes, that is a horrible thing: to wonder if the best or the worst will happen, and feel there is nothing that you can do about it. But how does Frederick *feel*? Does he fear the possibility of... of losing his sight?"

Gretchen sighed. "Yes, I do think so. You know how *little* he is prone to say, but it seems clear to me that he is devastated at the thought of losing his sight. I think that he is all the more determined to spend all his time composing and writing his music, you know, before he cannot see to do it. He is always upstairs playing: all the more than usual."

I offered, "But surely, if he could no longer see, he could still play. He could still compose."

"Yes, I certainly suppose he would. But I think he is worried about seeing, to write what he composes, you know."

I thought to suggest, in hoping to help with any idea, "He

could hire a scribe, you know, someone to *write* the music as he plays and composes it. Someone with a little knowledge of writing music could help him."

"But where would we find such a person out *here*?"

"Well, if nothing else, perhaps someone could be sent for? But I would think that there would be someone nearer who could help for very little money."

Gretchen stared off and away. "I suppose."

There was a still sadness looming, and we both felt it immensely.

42
Barriers

Gretchen had sent her husband home to his parents. He had pressing business to attend to back east and he simply could not stay protractedly. He wanted her to come with him, his parents were profoundly anxious to see their grandson, but she could not bring herself to leave until more was known of her brother's condition. She and the baby were staying a little longer. She felt her brother and her mother needed her, so she would stay.

For the musician, all thoughts of marrying me seemed gone forever. From what Gretchen had told me, talk between herself and Frederick on the subject of his ever marrying me (or anyone else, for that matter), had ceased. He would never wish to marry if he were to go blind. He could not comprehend being the blind husband. For now, he would simply wait to see what might happen with his headaches and to his sight. For now, he would just compose, and think of nothing else. Indeed, I had not seen him since Gretchen told me of his troubles. He kept entirely to his rooms upstairs.

Of course, you might imagine that I cared deeply about Frederick and the possibility of his going blind, and what that would mean to him: but I did not care so much as far as myself and loving him was concerned. I would not love him *less* because of such a limitation. No, I already loved him more *because* he might go blind. My compassion forced me to do so. I felt nothing but empathy for how he must feel at the thoughts of losing his sight and the way that condition would limit him. I could only imagine all the ways he would find difficulty, but I especially tried to comprehend how it would frustrate his composing of music. Frederick lived his music, and to him, living was composing. Without his sight, he would face much difficulty in continuing what was his life's work.

And so it was that Frederick kept entirely to his rooms to compose his music. Gretchen told me that he was pouring himself into his music all the more now. He would not come down for meals. He would not go for walks or any such thing. It was as if he feared that his time in life to compose was limited and so he threw himself into his work. He wanted to finish as much as he could, before it was too late, as he thought. And so it was also that the more he focused on his music, the more his headaches increased, and the more troubled was his sight. The fogginess of vision and the blinding episodes were still intermittent, but increasing in intensity or at least severity and especially in frequency. This was what Gretchen had explained to me.

Beyond Frederick's feelings about his discomfiting situation, I had feelings of my own. Of course I ached for Frederick's worries, his pain, his suffering, and what might become of him. Nevertheless, I also had my own children and our little life together to think of. The more I thought of it, the more I believed that I did not know how I could marry and take my children away from their dear Grandmother Ramstock in any case. She would seem lost without them. Even to take them a mile away would cause her such sadness. And what would such a change mean for my children as well? I could not help but put them first in my thoughts. I could not think of marrying without thinking of what that would mean for my children.

Well, I supposed all that pondering was of no account now. My children and I would stay with Grandmother Ramstock, and Frederick would play at his piano. The musician would compose as long as he was able to do so. I still believed that a scribe of sorts could be found. I felt assured that even if Frederick were to go blind, he could still compose, though perhaps not as efficiently, and somewhat beholding to someone who could help him. I sensed how that could frustrate him. I believed it would try his patience to depend upon another hand in the creating of his music.

I have to say that whenever I went to the Weiss house to visit, coming or going, in or out, I could hear the lamentation in Frederick's playing. He was suffering grievously. All he composed seemed sorrowful to me. There was such a sadness in his playing now. I wept for him, many times. Did I cry only for Frederick and what he was going through? No, my tears were also for myself, and the love I could have known with him. Yes, I ached to marry and love my dear Frederick. I felt a severe loss letting go of my musician.

43
Writing Music

Gretchen came early to my door. With an animation of felicity, she rushed me outside to speak privately, "We have a solution! My mother and I know what to do. *You* will act as musical scribe to Frederick! What do you say to that, Isabelle?"

I sorrowfully shook my head as I spoke, "No, I do not know how. How could I? I am a lowly pianist at best, and I do not know much about writing music. I barely read it, Gretchen. I cannot play or read music anywhere near Frederick's level. How could I possibly learn to write his music for him?"

"But Frederick will teach you. He will be patient enough with *you*, and I know you will be patient with him. He will teach you what you need to know while he can still see, and then, if the worst happens and he loses his sight, you will know what to do to help him write his music."

"Well, perhaps I can learn. Yes, I am sure that I could learn to write music if Frederick would teach me. But has he agreed to this? Does he truly want me to do this for him?"

"We have not spoken to him about it as yet. My mother and I decided that I should speak to you first before proceeding with the idea. We were lamenting about not knowing who could write Frederick's music for him and to work with him, and thinking that he would not like a stranger coming to help him, and suddenly, my mother mentioned you! The idea was pure inspiration! We are certain that *this* is the correct solution. This is the right course to take."

I was a little surprised. "But you have not spoken to Frederick about this idea? Are you sure that he would want me to work with him? Do you really think that he will agree to this?"

Gretchen smiled widely. "Oh, yes. Well, maybe he will resist at first. His pride and all, you know. He won't want you to sit with him in his condition, you know, that sort of thing. But, we will convince him. We will wear him down if need be. He simply *must* agree to this. He must teach you to write his music for him and then he must allow you to help him, you know, if it comes to that."

I felt deeply as I spoke, "Gretchen, I very much want to help Frederick in this. Indeed, I would wish to help him in any way that I could."

"And my mother will pay you."

I was taken aback at first and might have felt insulted if Gretchen was anyone else, and so I chose to measure my words very carefully, "I could not accept payment for helping Frederick write his music, Gretchen. After all that he means to me, I could *never* take payment for helping him with his music. You understand what I am saying, don't you?"

I thought that she felt the weight of what I tried to convey, "Oh yes, I am sorry for any hurt I might have caused you by blurting that out in that way. I do understand. You still love Frederick and you would willingly give freely of your time and efforts for him. I did not mean to offend you or to cheapen your willingness to give so freely to my brother. It is just that my mother did not wish to ask a free favor of you, because it would be quite an undertaking, you see. And she feels, and I think as well, that Frederick might only agree to this idea *if* you were paid for your work and time. A stranger would be paid in such a case, and so why would we not pay you?"

I was all seriousness, and full of feeling and painful honesty when I explained, "Gretchen, I still love your brother. In point of fact, I love him all the more now. You don't *know* how I worry about him every day; how he is feeling day to day, and what might happen to his sight. I fret about his headaches. I sorrow for his suffering. I worry over his health and even his very life. Truly, I wonder how he is doing my every waking hour. I ache for him. If I could help him in *any* way, even as only simply a friend, I would be relieved of some of my own suffering relative to him. Please do not speak of payment. I simply could not take payment for helping Frederick. I would not want my aiding him to be thought of as work. It would not be work to me. It would be my sincere privilege. I could only offer help as a true friend, but not the employed. Why could he not agree to this? I am certain that you can convince your mother. Please do not mention any matter of money when you suggest to Frederick that I will come and learn to write music so that I can later be his scribe while he composes, if ever he loses his sight and has need of my help."

"I will try, Isabelle, but I don't know that either my mother or Frederick will agree to this plan unless you are paid. I think that they would each feel equally ashamed to submit you to work in our house without your due payment."

I sighed and then thought to suggest, "Well, I have another way of thinking on the subject. Frederick would be teaching me something quite valuable. Some could argue that I should pay him for instructing me. We both know that your brother would not take payment from me for his teaching me to write music; and then if he ever had need of me to be his musical scribe as he composes, I should not take payment from him either. I would only be giving back with that which he had taught me."

Gretchen laughed and then had to agree, "When you put it all in that way, I suppose I can convince the two of them to bring you to help as a friend. Frederick will help you, and then you will be available to help him, if the need does eventually arise."

I suddenly was struck with a little revelation of clarification, "Yes, and you see, you will simply be proposing to Frederick that he teach me to read and write music. Is that not all you will be suggesting at first? If so, he could be convinced to think that the favor is all on his side. It will only possibly be later on, that any favor to him might be needed from me."

"Oh yes! Of course! It is all so very simple to begin with. I do think that I can at least convince them not to pay you for being taught to read and write music by Frederick. I cannot promise for the latter, for if he does need your help later on, you may need to accept some payment for that."

It was soon settled. I did not hear of all the details or minutiae of conversation that brought it all about. All I knew was that I was to come, and to come over regularly, to sit with Frederick and to learn how to read and write music from him. Gretchen had sincerely counseled me to never mention around or *to* Frederick that I might someday be needed to act as his scribe, or to let on that his teaching me now might be the first part of a larger favor on my side. For now, I was only to learn. It had all been posed as his favor to me. I wondered if Frederick even knew that I had ever been aware of his headaches and vision difficulties. I thought not. I did not care. I would be with him.

Once working with Frederick, in enjoyable moments day to day, during hours here and there learning many things about music from him; we were becoming all the more as two fast and fond friends. There was no hint towards marriage now, no intimation of love between us in any way. Yes, I still hoped to become his wife in future, but for now, I was happy simply to be his dear friend. Neither of us made any mention of anything akin to marriage, though I knew that my love for him was growing continually, and I did think that I could detect in him a greater love for me as well.

One of the first things that occurred to me in our times together, at the family piano (for not a one of us considered the improper shutting away of Frederick and myself, alone at his piano up in his room), was that Frederick did not drink enough water, stop to eat food regularly enough, nor take a little time away from the piano as I thought that he should. As he taught me the intricacies of writing music, I noticed that he was so entirely driven that he would forget all else. If nothing more, I, myself, would become thirsty, hungry and weary. And so, I forced Frederick to stop from time to time for any sustenance that I felt was needed.

I had quickly begun to wonder if Frederick's headaches, and even his weakened eyesight, since the two seemed connected, could fully be due to his not taking proper care of himself. As a mother, I knew how my children could not function well if they did not take nourishment and naps often enough. I also knew how ill I could begin to feel if I hungered and thirsted or was deprived of my sleep. I knew how working too long without a little respite in-between felt. I knew how blurry my vision seemed late at night when I was in dire need of sleep. Without saying a single thing to Frederick, or even to his sister or mother, I simply did my utmost to guide Frederick to greater balance of health. I reminded him to partake of a little sustenance now and then.

Letting my own needs be my guide, I would ask for moments of rations and rest. Frederick would happily comply, since he thought that we were breaking our work for me. He was perfectly amiable to stop teaching me so that I could drink or eat a little. And thus, he would drink and eat also. I would ask for a few moments away from the piano, and so Frederick would step away from it with me. I would ask for a little walk outside, and so he would walk out with me.

Perhaps I was using my female wiles a little, in order to make certain that Frederick did not go hungry or thirsty, and that he got a little fresh air and movement now and then, but such a slight manipulation seemed a completely worthwhile one to me. You see, I did not think that Frederick would be as inclined to stop our work at the piano for himself, as he was so easily persuaded for my own needs, and so I let him think that we were taking little breaks from the task for *my* sake, when it was just as often that I felt it was actually as much or more for his sake.

One afternoon, after luncheon, and then some little time at the piano, I had asked Frederick for a few turns around the Weiss yard. I felt the need for a stretch and was assured that the walking out of doors would do my dear friend a deal of good as well. Of course he graciously and instantly complied to my request.

Once outside, and as we began our walking together, he said to me, "You know, I am growing to like your little habits of stopping often to lunch or to take a stroll. I confess, I am badly inclined to sit too long at my work. You have taught me to step away from my work now and then, and I think it is doing me a world of good."

I replied, "Well, I suppose my little children have taught or reminded me that they cannot be too long at work or even play. They must stop for nourishment often. They must get their rest. And they cannot sit or stand still for long either. I have learned that this is true for me as well. I cannot be at my best and feel my best if I am always working. There must be a balance of work, of rest and of taking sustenance."

"Yes, that is exactly what I have been thinking. There must be a balance. I have not always had that. In fact, I have been quite abysmal at that sort of thing. I know that I tend to become obsessed with my work, and I am realizing that I have suffered for my narrow focus and dogged determination. Too often I do not feel well, and I do not even realize why. With you here so often, with you reminding me to stop and to step away from the piano, I have been feeling far better."

I wanted to ask him about his headaches, and of course I wondered about his eyesight; but I could not bring myself to broach those subjects. I still did not know if he knew that I was aware of these troubles and fears of his in recent months. I could not dare ask such things as yet. Even if I thought it appropriate, I would not have known what to say to him in any case. I hoped that he was fully faring better lately, but how could I ask him if he still thought that he might be going blind?

The thought occurred to me to at least ask this, "And when I am not here with you, do you take proper care of yourself? Do you drink and eat?"

He smiled down at me. "Well, of course I do far better when you are here with me. You are almost like my little conscience."

I could not but smile in return when asking, "Your little conscience?"

"Yes, Isabelle. You are my lovely little conscience, always

reminding me to do better."

I loved hearing the sound of my name on his lips, and I delighted at hearing him think of me as his lovely little conscience, though I brought myself back to seriousness, "But, Frederick, I am not always here to remind you to take proper care of yourself. You must be sure to remember to remind *yourself*. You *must* take every care of yourself."

"Well, I am learning to eat and drink more often, even when you are not here with me."

"And what of sleep? Do you sleep? Do you give yourself enough chance to sleep at night?"

"All right, I will try to do better there too."

I almost scolded, "Frederick, you cannot do your best if you do not get your rest."

"See there? See how you remind me to take better care of myself?"

"But Frederick, you must remind yourself always. *You* must constantly take care of yourself. I am not here so very much. *I* am not here to always remind you."

"All right, I will try to do far better, when you are not here."

"Frederick, *promise* me that you will."

"Yes, yes, I promise. I *will*." And then he laughed.

"Why are you laughing at me? I am quite serious."

"I'm not laughing at you. I simply find you so charming. You are such a sweet little beautiful conscience. I only wish you would be with me always."

"But I cannot be with you always, and that is why you must take better care of yourself. I worry about you, Frederick. I worry that you don't remember to eat, drink and rest when I am not here. That sort of forgetful thing is not good for your health."

"Perhaps you *should* always be here then? I need my little conscience always with me."

I thought him strangely teasing me, but I continued in my vein of seriousness, "But I can't. You know that I must be often with my children. I can only come here infrequently, and only a few hours at a time, at most."

There was a glint in his eyes when he proposed, "But they could come here, with you. You and they could always be here, with me."

"Frederick, I could not have my children under foot and in your mother's way, while you teach me things of music. Always? I could not come over so very much as I think you are suggesting."

He looked intently at me when illuminating, "Oh no, I did not mean *that* at all."

"What did you mean, then?" I did not know what he was about. It was not like him to tease in this way. I thought his manner odd today. I did not know quite what to say in return. Why was he talking such nonsense?

With a chuckle and much warmth in his voice, Frederick clarified, "My silly little conscience! Can't you understand me? Do you not know of what I am suggesting? I am asking if you would be my *wife!*"

I was all surprised amazement, "Your *wife*?!"

"Yes! Have we not almost hinted in that way in the recent past, or especially just now, today? Can I not now formally ask it of you?"

And then it all came out, for I could not help it, "But your headaches? And your vision? I thought that you should fear to marry me because you thought you might be going blind? Gretchen said that you would never marry me or anyone if you thought you might become blind."

He took my hand in his. "Well, I do not know what the future holds for my sickness or health. Who ever really *does* know these things, Isabelle? For now, I feel perfectly grand and I can see quite clearly. I want to marry you. I need you. I love you. You have been my cure, Isabelle. You nourish me even as you remind me to get nourishment. You give me rest. With you around, my headaches dissipate. With you near, I can see very well. To cure one is to cure the other, it seems. You have lightened my head, cleared my vision and beyond all of that, you have fully healed my heart. Yes, my little conscience, you are my great cure."

He paused a moment, still holding my hand and looking at me. He was likely waiting for some kind of a proper response from me. I dare say he hoped for rapturous smiles. I said nothing. I did not quite know what to say. I was trying to find the right words. My mind was a muddle with how it would all work. What of my children? Could we all truly live happily together in the Weiss home?

Amid my silence, he continued, "With my beautiful little conscience around, I remember to stop for luncheon, and thus I feel quite well. With you near me, I feel better than I have in years. Say you will marry me and then *always* be here to remind me to sleep each night as well?"

As I looked up to him with happy tears welling in my eyes, I was a mix of elation and anxiousness, "Oh yes, Frederick. I *do* love you so very much. But what do your parents think of this? Have you warned them of this possibility? I know Gretchen wishes our union, but, will your parents mind very much?"

He was all calming, "Actually, Isabelle, I think they will all be relieved to see me finally happy and settled with a woman such as you. They think you an angel, believe me, they *all* do."

"But will we live here, and with my children too? I cannot believe that your parents would want my children running about in their house. And poor dear Grandmother Ramstock will be devastated to lose her darlings to another house other than her own. Should you and I take a little place between the two houses? Could we ever afford to? And how will *you* do having to exercise constant patience for my little ones? You've never been a father before. I just worry over all these details, Frederick. It is very overwhelming for me, you see."

Frederick exhibited sudden though loving firmness, "Isabelle. We need not fuss over every detail now. All will be worked out. All will be well. You will see."

"Yes, but…"

He interrupted my attempt at more worrisome questions

by taking me into his arms and kissing me gently. All thoughts dissipated. Wonderful feelings overtook.

44
With His Child

All was arranged. All *was* well. There were adjustments for everyone, but nothing was insurmountable. The senior Mr. and Mrs. Weiss did their utmost to graciously accept my children and me into their home. Grandmother Ramstock was assured that she would continue to see a great deal of her grandchildren, and that she would play a vital role in their upbringing, just as she long had done. Mr. Ramstock senior was as he always was. I knew not what he thought, and he did not matter too much to me and mine.

Gretchen was a busy butterfly, flitting about to help with all our marriage arrangements. As you might guess, she cried the most at my wedding to her brother. Then, when it was all joyfully done and it was time for my handsome husband and I to take our little wedding journey; with many more tears of joy and farewell at her own parting from the rest of us, Gretchen was taken back home eastward, by her own beloved husband and with their little son.

Grandmother Ramstock kept my children while Frederick and I enjoyed our blissful honeymoon weeks together. When my new husband and I came back to retrieve my children, and to have them move into their new home with us, our little ones seemed ready for anything. They surprised me by being adventurously delighted at the prospect of this enormous change. There were no tears about leaving their grandmother Ramstock, as I had feared that there might be. No, I suppose I had reassured them enough for them to know that they could see her almost any time they liked, and that they would certainly be over there almost as much as had been usual. They truly felt the addition of new loved ones and a new home, rather than any losses.

I did not fully comprehend the change because I had not been a visitor upstairs in the Weiss home, but from what I had been given to understand, Frederick had turned his set of upper rooms almost upside down, in preparation for my children and I to come live there with him. It quickly became obvious to me that Frederick wished to make certain that Lorna, Alan and I felt entirely welcome and perfectly at home, as instantly as he could make possible for us. Frederick confessed that he had cleaned up his own personal space of rooms a great deal, that such tidying was long overdue in any case, and thus it was no extra inconvenience for him to move a few things around to make way for a wife and two children. What an angelic man.

Shortly after Frederick and I had returned from our leisurely trip, and my children and I had moved upstairs into the Weiss family house, Frederick's parents announced that they were going to take their own little journey. They wished to visit some folks and friends back east, and it seemed that they planned to be gone quite extendedly. Mrs. Weiss particularly confessed to me that since she knew that her son was in my very capable and good hands, she felt free to indulge herself in a lengthy retreat away.

In the end, that trip of Frederick's parents turned into a more permanent thing. The elder Mr. and Mrs. Weiss took a little home of their own near Gretchen. Mrs. Weiss especially missed her little grandson Douglas, whom she had grown so used to holding, but she also wanted to be closer to her daughter. The older Weiss couple's overall plan was to live a good deal there near Gretchen, and also to live a little here with Frederick. What became of all this was that Frederick's parents ultimately gave their lovely home to him. We were to keep a room for them to stay in whenever they wished to come visit, but, other than that, we were to wholly settle into the house ourselves and call it our own.

And what were we to do for money to live on otherwise?

There were investments that gave us an adequate income through Frederick's father, and we could do work as we liked to supplement that. As the town grew, I could take in more dressmaking if I liked. Frederick could utilize his music a little for money, though our neighborhood terrain was a little rustic as yet to fully appreciate his abilities.

I wondered if we might someday move eastward to give Frederick more opportunities to advance his musical art. But this would take the children away from their beloved grandmother, and them away from her. Another, perhaps easier proposition was offered to my husband by way of his father and others that the family knew. We could occasionally go east and even to Europe, where Frederick would perform in concerts and perhaps even go on extended tours with his compositions of music. Such could be very profitable and also adventurous to us.

But for now, I had something else to distract my beloved husband with and to tell him, "Frederick? Now that you are getting so used to there being the four of us, what do you say to *five* as a nicely rounded number?"

He looked at me lovingly, his eyes wet with happy emotion. "Isabelle? Are you telling me that *you* will soon be rounded? You are to make me a father of three then?"

I smiled broadly. "Why yes, I certainly am."

He caressed me at length and then, "I shall write a song for our new son. What shall his name be, do you think?"

I took and held his face tenderly in my hands and countered teasingly, "You might want to write a song for another daughter. I already have a list of names for girls to show you. Would you like to see it now?"

He laughed and held me close to him, as he whispered in my ear, "I suppose I must draw up a list of boys' names to show *you* then? We shall have many a conference on the matter I suppose, but never any quarrel?"

I drank in the fragrance of his neck and whispered in return, "If 'tis a boy, you choose, if 'tis a girl, I choose? What say you to *that* notion?"

He pulled away to smile and say, "That would suit me just fine. Well, and while you create this child for us, I shall create two songs, because, boy or girl; for either blessing, I will thank the Heavens above even as I thank for you, my angel on earth. You, my dear, are all perfection."

I kissed my musician, and then asked him to play our song for me. Of course, he lovingly complied.

Made in the USA
Charleston, SC
01 April 2011